GHOSTS OF TH CITY

This is a work of fiction. Similarities to real people, places, or events are entirely coincidental.

GHOSTS OF THE GOLDEN CITY

First edition. November 15, 2024.

Copyright © 2024 Sibusiso Anthon Mkhwanazi.

ISBN: 979-8227050915

Written by Sibusiso Anthon Mkhwanazi.

Also by Sibusiso Anthon Mkhwanazi

Million-Dollar Decade
Resilience Beyond Pain
Resonance Of Hope
Cheating hearts to true love
The Dream Builders Of Daveyton
Before the Bible
Ink and Imagination
Becoming A Millionaire In South Africa
Leaders of the World
Mining In Africa
Origins of Language and Civilization
Vita Nova Centre
Sisters of A cursed bloodline
Witchcraft in Africa
Ghosts of the golden city

Table of Contents

SIBUSISO ANTHON MKHWANAZI 1
Chapter 1: Daveyton Beginnings 3
Chapter 2: Meet the Geniuses 7
Chapter 3: The First Heist 11
Chapter 4: Crafting Identities 15
Chapter 5: Signature Moves 21
Chapter 6: Building a Code 26
Chapter 7: The Financial Upsurge 29
Chapter 8: The Perfect Heist 34
Chapter 9: The Electronic Takeover 39
Chapter 10: Influencing the Influencers 43
Chapter 11: Money Talks 47
Chapter 12: The Johannesburg Lockdown 50
Chapter 13: Community Investment Begins 54
Chapter 14: Public Robin Hoods 58
Chapter 15: The Biggest Score Yet 62
Chapter 16: The Unbreakable Network 66
Chapter 17: Close Call 70
Chapter 18: The Cape Town Expansion 74
Chapter 19: International Allies 78
Chapter 20: High Society 82
Chapter 21: Ultimate Betrayal 86
Chapter 22: The Clandestine Operation 89
Chapter 23: Johannesburg's Benefactors 93
Chapter 24: Heist Unraveled 97
Chapter 25: Covering Tracks 101
Chapter 26: Uplifting SA's Future 105
Chapter 27: Blurring the Line 108
Chapter 28: A City in Their Pockets 111
Chapter 29: The Final Operation 115
Chapter 30: Legacy Left Behind 118

SIBUSISO ANTHON MKHWANAZI

Dedication
To those who dare to defy the odds,
who find light in the darkest corners,
and who believe that even the most broken systems
can be reshaped for good.
And to Johannesburg—its heartbeat, resilience,
and the untold stories it holds.

PART 1: ORIGINS OF Vuruvayi and His Circle

Chapter 1: Daveyton Beginnings

THE NARROW STREETS of Daveyton buzzed with life. Shouts of children echoed through alleyways, a symphony of laughter, distant music, and the hum of vendors calling out their wares. The township was rough around the edges, a place of resilience where everyone hustled to survive. Amidst this energy, Vuruvayi grew up with a mind sharp as a blade, molded by the heat of adversity.

Vuruvayi's mother, Thandeka, was a force of nature. She could cook, sew, and work with her hands in ways that earned her respect among the neighbors. But life wasn't easy. She worked day and night to keep food on the table, sewing clothes for wealthier families during the day and making steaming pots of chakalaka and pap to sell in the evenings. Vuruvayi often watched her, amazed at her endurance but also saddened by her weary face, etched with lines from years of struggle.

"Ma," he'd asked her one night while she was stitching yet another torn shirt, "why do we have to work so hard just to survive?"

She looked up, pausing, her hands roughened by years of labor resting momentarily on her lap. "Because, my boy, this world doesn't give us anything for free. You take what you can get, or you get nothing at all."

That lesson stuck with him. From a young age, Vuruvayi learned to make do with what little he had. He became the leader among his friends, gathering up scraps of wood and metal to build makeshift toys or scrounging for food. Together, they survived. He had a way of guiding them, a natural charm that inspired loyalty. If there was trouble, his friends knew they could count on Vuruvayi to find a way out.

In school, Vuruvayi's teachers noticed his spark. He was bright, quicker than most, and often found clever ways to solve problems. But Daveyton was a place that tested patience. Opportunities were rare, and even the smartest kids often found themselves caught in the cycle of poverty. Vuruvayi felt the weight of that truth settle into his bones with every passing year.

As he grew older, his eyes were opened to the harsh reality around him. Some of his friends dropped out of school, while others were pulled into petty crime to support their families. He knew he could end up on the same path if he wasn't careful. It was one thing to steal to fill an empty stomach; it was another to live that way forever.

But poverty wasn't Vuruvayi's only teacher. Daveyton had its share of under-the-radar dealers, loan sharks, and hustlers—people who had found ways to make the system work for them. They lived differently, not bound by the rules that everyone else seemed forced to follow. Vuruvayi saw them drive nice cars, wear fancy clothes, and get away with things that would land others in jail. He saw the respect people gave them, though it was often muttered in hushed tones, and he began to wonder: what if the only way to win was to rewrite the rules?

When he was sixteen, Vuruvayi had his first brush with crime. He didn't set out to become a thief; it just happened. Hunger gnawed at his stomach, and as he passed by a shop with fresh bread on display, something inside him snapped. In a quick, impulsive move, he snatched a loaf and ran, the thrill of adrenaline pumping through his veins. That night, as he ate the stolen bread, he felt a strange satisfaction, not just from filling his stomach but from the idea that, in some way, he had beaten the system.

Yet Vuruvayi didn't just want to survive; he wanted to thrive. He wasn't content with scraps or handouts. In his mind, a vision began to form—a life free from the shackles of poverty, a life where he could provide not only for himself but for the people around him. To do that, he needed more than just courage; he needed allies.

And as fate would have it, he began to meet the right people. There was Dumi, a wiry young man with a gift for numbers, who could make money appear and disappear with the stroke of a pen. Then there was Linda, quiet and unassuming, but with a mind sharp enough to hack into government databases for fun. Tumi was the brawn of the group, tough and relentless, with a knack for planning and logistics that could rival any military strategist. Each of them had dreams beyond the township, dreams as big and uncontained as his own.

Together, they would sit late into the night, talking about the life they wanted, the lives they deserved. And slowly, a plan took shape. It was a dangerous plan, one that could either lead them to fortune or land them in jail for the rest of their lives. But for Vuruvayi, the decision was already made. He wasn't going to let himself or his friends become victims of a world that offered them no second chances.

One night, as they gathered in a darkened corner of an abandoned building, Vuruvayi looked at each of them, his eyes burning with determination. "If we're going to make it out of here, we need to be smart. We take only from those who won't miss it and use what we gain to build something real, something that can't be taken away."

His friends listened, their faces lit only by the faint glow of a single, flickering candle. In that moment, a pact was formed—a pact to rise above, to outsmart the world that had tried to trap them. They were more than friends now; they were a team, bound by loyalty and a hunger for something better.

Thus began Vuruvayi's journey, from a child of the township to the mastermind of a team whose cunning and skills would eventually leave their mark across Johannesburg. But for now, they were just a group of ambitious youth with a plan, a dream, and a fierce determination to carve out a destiny that belonged to them alone.

Chapter 2: Meet the Geniuses

DAVEYTON HAD A WAY of bringing people together. Life here had a rhythm, a heartbeat that pulsed through every street and corner, uniting the people in shared struggles and rare victories. Amid this tough reality, Vuruvayi found his crew—his brothers and sisters in arms, each possessing a skill that made them not only essential to the team but invaluable to his vision.

Dumi - The Financial Wizard

Dumi was the first to join Vuruvayi's circle. Lanky and wiry, with an uncanny way of melting into the background, Dumi was quiet yet sharp. He had a talent with numbers that bordered on supernatural. He could take one look at a bank statement and tell you exactly where the money was coming from, how it was being funneled, and how it could be rerouted without anyone ever noticing.

Vuruvayi had met him outside a shebeen, where Dumi had been selling a makeshift budgeting service to locals, helping them manage their limited funds. Dumi could stretch a rand in ways that left even the most frugal adults speechless. Vuruvayi watched him work, fascinated, until Dumi noticed him and cracked a smile.

"What's up, Vuru? Need help with your cash flow?" Dumi asked, grinning.

Vuruvayi chuckled, sensing an unspoken connection. "Nah, but I could use someone who knows how to handle money."

They struck up a conversation, which turned into an all-night discussion about money laundering, offshore accounts, and even cryptocurrency. Dumi had learned it all from library books and the internet, a self-taught financial prodigy who saw the world as one big system waiting to be outsmarted. Vuruvayi knew then that he had found his first genius.

Linda - The Tech Prodigy

Linda was next. She was an enigma, known around town as the girl who could make anything digital bend to her will. Slim and quiet, she kept to herself, preferring the company of her laptop to that of people. Vuruvayi met her by accident, in a cramped internet café where she was typing away, face illuminated by the glow of the screen.

He struck up a conversation, intrigued by the code running across her screen. Linda, wary at first, eventually warmed up, revealing her talent for hacking. She could bypass passwords, access secured data, and even crack Wi-Fi networks. With a mix of curiosity and caution, she allowed Vuruvayi a peek into her world. Linda could bring down systems, disable cameras, and dig up information on anyone—all from a single computer.

As their friendship grew, Vuruvayi became fascinated by her work. He saw in Linda the power to navigate the digital world in ways that most people couldn't imagine. She was a ghost online, invisible yet unstoppable. Together, they crafted ways to use her skills to protect the team and even enhance their "business" when the time came.

BHEKA - THE MASTER of Psychology

Then there was Bheka, the quiet, thoughtful one. Unlike the others, Bheka was a true people person, not because he enjoyed socializing but because he understood how people thought. Tall and calm, he could read anyone, picking up on subtle cues and hints that most people missed. His gift was knowing exactly how to make people trust him, how to say the right thing at the right time, and how to make anyone believe his every word.

Vuruvayi met Bheka during a heated argument outside a township tuck shop. Bheka, without raising his voice, had calmed the crowd and defused the tension in minutes, simply by understanding what each person needed to hear. Afterward, Vuruvayi approached him, curious about how he'd done it.

"It's all about people, Vuru," Bheka explained, shrugging. "Everyone wants something. You just have to figure out what that is."

Bheka's skills were less tangible than Dumi's or Linda's, but they were equally valuable. He could persuade almost anyone to do almost anything, a quality that would become crucial in navigating the social and political networks of Johannesburg's underground. He was a natural mediator and manipulator, able to win over friends and enemies alike with a simple conversation.

TUMI - THE LOGISTICS Genius

Finally, there was Tumi. Broad-shouldered, with a commanding presence, Tumi was the planner, the one who could map out routes, time schedules, and escape plans down to the second. He was the only one of the group who had tried to stay out of trouble, working odd jobs and focusing on his studies. But life in Daveyton didn't leave much room for dreams, and he was often frustrated with his lack of options.

Vuruvayi saw potential in Tumi that even Tumi didn't see in himself. They met after a community soccer game, where Tumi's strategies on the field had left everyone in awe. Intrigued, Vuruvayi invited him for a drink, where they discussed the importance of timing, organization, and precision.

"You know, if you can plan a game, you can plan a heist," Vuruvayi said, half-joking but watching Tumi's reaction closely.

At first, Tumi had laughed, thinking it was all in jest. But the more they talked, the more he realized that he had a natural talent for orchestrating complex plans. Before long, he joined the crew, bringing a skill set that would prove invaluable. With Tumi at the helm of logistics, no detail was overlooked, no escape route unplanned.

THE BONDS THAT BOUND Them

As they spent more time together, their bond deepened. Each of them brought something unique to the table, a skill that the others couldn't replicate, creating a balance that made them stronger together than they could ever be alone. They spent countless nights strategizing, dreaming, and daring each other to imagine a life beyond their township.

In quiet moments, they shared their stories, their dreams, and their fears. They were more than just friends; they became a family. In each other, they found acceptance, strength, and trust. They knew that, if they stuck together, they could take on anything the world threw at them.

For Vuruvayi, this crew was more than just a team; they were his hope, his strength, and his answer to the injustices he'd grown up with. They were a mix of brains, heart, and brawn, ready to carve out a new path and take on a system that had always tried to keep them down.

In the glow of flickering streetlights, they made a pact. This wasn't about revenge, or simple survival. This was about rewriting their story. In that moment, they became something more—a team that would soon become infamous across Johannesburg, a team led by Vuruvayi, the man with a plan and a heart as fierce as fire.

Chapter 3: The First Heist

IT WAS A BRISK, QUIET night in Johannesburg, with only the hum of traffic and the distant sounds of the city breaking the silence. The crew sat crammed in Dumi's beat-up sedan, parked in the shadows a few blocks away from their target—a cash-in-transit truck scheduled to stop at a rundown ATM for a routine deposit. The job was small-scale, but for Vuruvayi and his team, this was the first real test of their skills.

Vuruvayi looked around at his friends. Dumi was in the driver's seat, hands gripping the wheel, his leg bouncing with nervous energy. Linda sat in the back, laptop open, fingers flying over the keys as she hacked into the truck's GPS, keeping them informed of its location. Bheka was beside her, calm and collected, running through their cover story in case things went wrong. Tumi, positioned right next to Vuruvayi, had mapped out their entry and exit down to the last detail.

"This is it, guys," Vuruvayi said, his voice steady, though his heart pounded. "We stick to the plan. In and out. No improvising unless absolutely necessary."

The others nodded, the weight of their first job settling over them.

Linda spoke up, eyes glued to her screen. "They're three minutes out. We've got a fifteen-second window once they're at the ATM."

Bheka leaned forward, his voice calm as ever. "Remember, confidence is everything. We walk like we belong, we act like we've done this a hundred times."

The truck was getting closer. Vuruvayi adjusted his baseball cap and gave a nod to Tumi, who responded with a quick thumbs-up. They were ready.

THE SETUP

The target was a small cash delivery intended for an off-site ATM, handled by a private security company with lax protocols. It wasn't the most lucrative job, but it was perfect for their first heist—low stakes, high reward, and an opportunity to test their coordination.

As planned, the truck pulled up to the ATM at exactly 11:32 p.m. Two guards stepped out, each holding a bag, one containing cash and the other equipment to service the ATM. Their movements were routine, almost bored; they'd done this a hundred times before. That's when the crew made their move.

Vuruvayi, Bheka, and Tumi approached from the left, calm but purposeful. Dumi stayed in the car, engine running, while Linda monitored from a safe distance, ready to disrupt any alarms if needed.

Bheka, with his talent for reading people, led the approach. He walked up to the first guard, who instinctively tensed, his hand going to his holster. But Bheka was ready.

"Hey there, officer," he said in a tone that was light yet firm. "We're from the municipal inspection team. Routine check-up on cash delivery security. Quick and easy—just need a minute of your time."

The guard relaxed, caught off guard by Bheka's authority and calm demeanor. "I wasn't informed of any inspection," the guard muttered, frowning.

"Yeah, well, management likes to keep things on the down-low," Bheka said with a friendly shrug. "You know how it is. We're almost done here. Just need your partner over here too."

The guard, disoriented by Bheka's easy confidence, called over his partner, who was fumbling with the ATM. As the two men stood together, Vuruvayi nodded to Tumi, who stepped forward and subtly disabled the guard's radio, pretending to inspect it.

"Ah, looks like you've got some interference," Tumi said, flashing a knowing smile at Vuruvayi. "This could take a while."

THE HEIST UNFOLDS

With the guards distracted, Vuruvayi moved swiftly, signaling Linda through a discreet earpiece. In seconds, she hacked into the ATM's operating system, temporarily disabling the alarms and security cameras. She whispered over the line, "You're good to go, but you have two minutes before the system resets."

Bheka kept the guards occupied, asking questions and feigning interest in their routines, while Vuruvayi and Tumi seized the opportunity. Tumi quickly unlatched the cash compartment, slipping the bills into a duffel bag with practiced efficiency. The pile of crisp, green notes grew in seconds.

"Time's almost up," Linda's voice crackled in their earpieces, bringing a sense of urgency to the air.

Vuruvayi glanced back at the guards, making sure they were still under Bheka's spell. Then, with a final nod to Tumi, he whispered, "Let's go."

They moved smoothly, slipping back toward the car without drawing attention. Bheka wrapped up his conversation with the guards, thanking them for their cooperation and handing back the disabled radio as if it were no big deal.

"Have a safe night, gents," he said, flashing them a casual smile. The guards, still none the wiser, returned to the ATM as the crew slipped back to the car, duffel bag in hand.

Dumi barely waited for them to shut the doors before he floored the gas, the sedan peeling away from the curb and into the

Johannesburg night. They drove in silence, hearts pounding, each of them processing what had just happened.

BACK AT BASE

When they reached their hideout, a small, unassuming storage unit rented under a false name, the adrenaline finally began to subside. Vuruvayi dumped the duffel bag on the floor, and they all gathered around, eyes wide with excitement and disbelief. They'd done it.

Linda looked at Vuruvayi, a grin spreading across her face. "Not bad for a first heist, huh?"

Vuruvayi couldn't help but smile back. "Not bad at all. But we've got a long way to go."

They counted the money—ten thousand rand. It wasn't a fortune, but it was a start. Each of them held a stack of bills, letting the reality of their success sink in. They'd outsmarted the guards, bypassed the system, and pulled off a flawless heist.

As they celebrated, Dumi raised a bottle of cheap beer, his eyes gleaming with pride. "To the beginning of something big."

They all toasted, the clinking of bottles marking a milestone in their journey. They knew this was just the beginning. The taste of victory was addictive, the rush of adrenaline exhilarating. But more than the money or the thrill, it was the bond they shared—the trust, the teamwork—that made this moment so powerful.

As they sat around, talking about the future, Vuruvayi looked at each of his friends, the thrill still buzzing in his veins. This was what he had always wanted: a crew he could trust, a family of misfits bound together by a common goal. And he knew that as long as they had each other, there was no limit to what they could accomplish.

They were ready for more, for bigger jobs, and they had the skills to back it up. They had tested the waters, and now, they were prepared to dive deeper.

Chapter 4: Crafting Identities

IN THE DIM LIGHT OF their hideout, the team gathered around a worn-out table scattered with notebooks, laptops, and stacks of fake IDs. The adrenaline from their first heist had barely faded, but Vuruvayi knew that if they were to aim higher, they needed to be prepared. They couldn't go around Johannesburg as themselves. They needed new names, new faces, and new stories—identities that could withstand scrutiny.

Vuruvayi cleared his throat, his tone serious. "From now on, the stakes get higher. We need to blend in, slip under the radar. If anyone asks, we're just regular people going about our business. But to do that, each of us needs a cover—something that can hold up if we're questioned."

Each of them nodded, fully aware that the next level required a transformation.

DUMI - THE ACCOUNTANT

Dumi adjusted his glasses, his mind already racing with possibilities. Vuruvayi had tasked him with the role of financial genius, and while that was already his natural strength, he needed an alias that could get him inside financial institutions, places they couldn't access as themselves.

He leaned back, thinking aloud. "Alright, I'll be Thabo Maseko, a freelance accountant from Soweto. Specialized in tax filings for small businesses."

Vuruvayi nodded approvingly. "Thabo Maseko. Has a ring to it. You'll need credentials, though. Can you create a digital trail?"

Dumi grinned, already pulling out his laptop. "Give me a few hours, and Thabo Maseko will have a clean history of transactions, tax returns, even a LinkedIn profile. If anyone searches, they'll find enough to believe he's legit."

Linda chimed in, "I can help with that. I'll use a few social media tricks to give Thabo some professional contacts and endorsements."

As Dumi and Linda worked together, Vuruvayi felt a sense of pride. They were not only creating new identities but building entire personas, ones that could blend into the corporate world and get them access to financial resources and secure institutions.

LINDA - THE IT CONSULTANT

Next up was Linda, who was already skilled at keeping herself hidden in the digital world. But if they were going to infiltrate high-tech security systems, she needed to present herself as someone with the right expertise.

"I'll be Lerato Khoza," she said, smiling. "IT consultant and cybersecurity expert. I'll keep it vague—enough to explain my skills without raising suspicion. People like Lerato don't usually work in offices, so I'll be a freelancer, working for companies all over Gauteng."

Vuruvayi nodded thoughtfully. "That's smart. Gives you a reason to be anywhere, anytime. And you're good at the freelance thing; no one will ask questions."

Linda laughed, her fingers dancing across her keyboard as she created accounts, filled out fake employment histories, and even registered an official business profile for "Lerato Khoza – IT Solutions."

By the end of the evening, Lerato Khoza had a track record, a portfolio, and a client list, thanks to Linda's digital sleight of hand.

BHEKA - THE COMMUNITY Advocate

Bheka's role was trickier. His strength lay in understanding and manipulating people, a skill that couldn't be easily hidden behind a desk job. He needed an identity that allowed him to move through neighborhoods, approach people, and gain trust without raising suspicion.

"How about a community worker?" Bheka suggested, rubbing his chin. "I'll be Sipho Dlamini, from a local NGO that helps township youth with job placement and mentorship programs. That way, I can be anywhere without people questioning me."

Vuruvayi raised an eyebrow, impressed. "Sipho Dlamini...a mentor. That's perfect. People will naturally want to trust you."

Bheka took a moment to practice his new persona, straightening his posture and softening his expression. "I can run workshops, host meetings in community centers. People will come to me. It'll give us an ear to the ground in the neighborhoods, too—if something's happening, I'll be the first to know."

To back up Sipho's credibility, Linda crafted a simple but professional website for his "organization," filling it with photos of Bheka helping groups of young people, his face always calm and trustworthy.

TUMI - THE TRANSPORT Specialist

Tumi's role required a careful touch. He needed to be the logistical mastermind, a person who knew Johannesburg's streets better than anyone. He would be the one planning their escapes, arranging routes, and acquiring vehicles without attracting attention.

"I'll go by Andile Khumalo, a delivery driver for a big courier company," Tumi said, after a moment of thought. "Delivery drivers know all the best routes, shortcuts, and times to avoid traffic. No one would think twice if they saw me parked somewhere or leaving a warehouse."

Vuruvayi liked the idea. "And if we ever need to move equipment or cash, Andile could be the guy driving the van. No one will suspect a thing."

Tumi spent the next few days familiarizing himself with delivery routes, memorizing schedules, and adding personal touches to his "Andile Khumalo" persona. He even bought a worn uniform from an old delivery service, making his disguise look authentic down to the last detail.

VURUVAYI - THE STRATEGIST

Finally, it was Vuruvayi's turn. He needed a persona that allowed him to lead without being noticed—a low-profile strategist who could blend in while still commanding respect when necessary.

"I'll be Themba Ndlovu," he decided. "A low-key project manager who oversees logistics for small businesses."

The job was ordinary, mundane even. But it gave Vuruvayi the authority to make quick decisions, delegate tasks, and direct people without drawing suspicion. Themba Ndlovu was organized, confident, and calm—a leader, but one who preferred to stay in the background.

Dumi gave a nod of approval. "Themba Ndlovu sounds like someone who knows what he's doing but isn't out to be the center of attention. It suits you."

With the identity in place, Vuruvayi created a paper trail that showed "Themba" working with various businesses around Johannesburg, managing supply chains, and solving logistical problems.

THE FINAL TEST

With their new identities in place, the crew ran drills, practicing how they'd answer questions, respond to situations, and carry themselves in their new roles. They practiced in public, interacting with locals, buying supplies, even attending small events where they could blend in and get a feel for their new lives.

Each member adopted their new persona so thoroughly that they began referring to one another by their aliases, even when alone. Bheka became Sipho, the NGO worker. Linda was Lerato, the IT consultant. Dumi turned into Thabo, the financial advisor. Tumi embraced the role of Andile, the delivery driver. And Vuruvayi slipped seamlessly into the calm and calculated Themba.

Through trial and error, they learned the art of disguise, the subtle mannerisms that made their identities convincing. They'd built not only fake lives but entire backgrounds, personal quirks, and traits that made their new personas feel real. They'd even mapped out small biographical details—favorite foods, hometowns, education—to make sure their stories would hold up under questioning.

The final test came one Saturday when they decided to introduce themselves, as their new identities, to some unsuspecting locals. They chose a small community event in Johannesburg, where "Sipho" handed out pamphlets about his youth program, "Thabo" spoke to residents about financial planning, and "Lerato" offered tech advice. Andile and Themba stayed in the background, playing the supporting roles.

By the end of the event, the crew had proven to themselves that they could blend in, earning nods of approval from strangers who had no idea they were speaking to a crew of masterminds. Each persona held up under casual scrutiny, and each member had settled into their roles like a second skin.

A NEW ERA BEGINS

When they regrouped that night, the thrill of success was tangible. They had accomplished the first part of Vuruvayi's vision, becoming invisible in plain sight. With these identities, they could move freely, access places previously off-limits, and execute more complex heists without raising suspicion.

As they sat around, the usual hum of excitement filling the air, Vuruvayi raised a toast. "To new beginnings—and new identities. From here on out, we are whoever we say we are. And with these lives, we'll take this city by storm."

The others echoed his words, their glasses clinking together. They knew this was just the beginning, but with their newfound identities, they felt invincible. As far as the world was concerned, Sipho, Lerato, Thabo, Andile, and Themba were just five ordinary people going about their lives in Johannesburg. But in reality, they were the core of a heist team destined to make history.

Chapter 5: Signature Moves

BACK AT THEIR HIDEOUT, the team was deep in planning mode. The success of their first heist had shown them what they were capable of, but Vuruvayi knew that if they were going to scale up, they needed to refine their individual skills. Each member had a unique talent that set them apart, and tonight was about showcasing those talents, brainstorming, and developing signature moves that would become their go-to strategies for future heists.

DUMI - THE FINANCIAL Mastermind

Dumi sat down with a pen and notepad, the dim light casting shadows on his face as he worked through complex financial projections. His talent wasn't just in understanding numbers; he could read economic patterns and make quick calculations in his head, a skill that proved invaluable when planning heists with high financial stakes.

"Alright," Dumi began, flipping his notebook open. "Let's talk cash flow and investments. When we pull off bigger heists, we'll need ways to move the money without raising alarms. I'm talking fake accounts, offshore investments, and clean channels for laundering. But first, we'll start small—like funneling our initial earnings through local small businesses."

The team listened intently as Dumi explained how, by spreading their money across multiple low-profile ventures, they could avoid suspicion while earning legitimate returns. He'd already identified a few small businesses in Johannesburg where they could quietly invest, creating a stable front that allowed them to manage and move funds without attracting attention.

He grinned, his eyes gleaming with ambition. "This way, our cash isn't just sitting around. It'll be working for us."

LINDA - THE DIGITAL Phantom

Next up was Linda, her fingers already tapping away on her laptop as she outlined her plan. She had always been able to slip into systems undetected, accessing and disabling security measures with ease. Now, she wanted to take it up a notch.

Linda turned her screen to face the others. "For the next job, I'll create ghost identities. Not just for us, but for anyone who might be on-site or who we may need as scapegoats. By creating fake records in their systems, I can give us extra protection. If anyone tries to trace us, they'll end up with a dead end or be led in circles."

She typed quickly, bringing up a demonstration of how she'd hacked into a local mall's CCTV network. With a few clicks, she showed them how she'd rerouted the live feeds to show empty halls, despite people moving around. For their upcoming heists, she planned to go a step further by creating real-time illusions—altering the footage as they moved, so no one watching would ever catch a glimpse of them.

"And if they do find anything," she added with a smirk, "it'll be a trail that ends at some unfortunate soul who has no idea what hit them."

BHEKA - THE MASTER of Persuasion

Bheka leaned forward, his voice calm and assured. Unlike the others, he didn't rely on gadgets or tools. His weapon was his ability to influence people, to read their emotions and exploit their weaknesses. His role in each heist was to control the human factor, making sure anyone they encountered felt at ease, convinced, or even intimidated when necessary.

"I'll play the face of the operation," Bheka said, his tone smooth. "When we need someone distracted or misled, leave it to me. I can create diversions, strike up conversations, even gather information without anyone suspecting a thing."

He demonstrated by sharing an example from their first heist, when he'd approached the guards, slipping into his role as "Sipho" with ease. He knew when to press, when to ease off, and how to pick up on cues from people around him. With this skill, Bheka could buy the crew the time they needed or steer attention away from sensitive areas.

"Give me ten minutes with anyone," he said confidently, "and I'll have them believing whatever I want."

TUMI - THE LOGISTICS Guru

Tumi, known for his knack for logistics, had spent weeks studying Johannesburg's streets, memorizing escape routes, alleyways, and traffic patterns. His job wasn't just to get them from point A to B, but to do so with precision, ensuring their movements were swift and undetectable.

"Timing and precision are everything," he began, spreading out a map of Johannesburg. "I've mapped out every major and minor road in the areas we'll be hitting. For each job, I'll plan the escape routes, timing them down to the second. This way, we'll avoid traffic, police, and any surveillance hot spots."

He tapped on certain sections of the map, showing various exits and hidden back roads they could use. Tumi also brought up a series of tools he'd be using to stay one step ahead—police scanners, GPS tracking, and even a coded system of signals that would let the team know if they needed to change routes on the fly.

"When things go sideways, I'll have backup routes ready," he added. "If we stick to the plan, we'll be ghosts by the time anyone knows we were there."

VURUVAYI - THE STRATEGIST

Finally, it was Vuruvayi's turn. As the strategist, his role was to bring it all together, using his friends' skills to create seamless, foolproof plans. He studied each heist from multiple angles, running through scenarios, calculating risks, and designing contingencies for every possible setback.

"My job is to anticipate every outcome, every detail," Vuruvayi said, his voice calm and calculating. "Before we even step on-site, I'll have the entire plan mapped out. I want each of us to know our roles inside out, so when things start moving, we're unstoppable."

He outlined a few scenarios for upcoming jobs, explaining how they would rotate roles if one of them got compromised, or how they could improvise on the spot without losing sight of the big picture. His strategic mind was relentless, always thinking three steps ahead, ensuring there were no gaps, no overlooked details.

Vuruvayi's goal was simple: to create plans so precise that even the most seasoned detectives would be left scratching their heads.

PUTTING IT ALL TOGETHER

With each member contributing their skills, the team felt stronger and more prepared than ever. They ran simulations, practicing each step of their next heist until it felt as natural as breathing. They worked tirelessly, running through drills, tweaking plans, and refining every aspect of their approach.

By the end of the night, each member had a signature move—a skill they had mastered and adapted for their heist work. Dumi's financial maneuvers, Linda's digital finesse, Bheka's persuasion, Tumi's logistical genius, and Vuruvayi's overarching strategy blended together like pieces of a well-oiled machine.

As they packed up, Vuruvayi looked around at his team, feeling a surge of pride and excitement.

"From now on, we don't just play the game," he said, his voice filled with conviction. "We control it."

Chapter 6: Building a Code

AS DAWN BROKE OVER Johannesburg, casting soft hues across the city, Vuruvayi and his crew gathered once again at their hideout. They had perfected their skills and created new identities, and now their ambitions were pointed toward something bigger. But Vuruvayi felt there was one thing left to solidify before they moved forward—a code that would define not only their targets but also the purpose behind each heist.

They all settled around the table, the usual hum of excitement dimmed by the serious expression on Vuruvayi's face.

"We've got the skills, the plans, and the grit to do anything," Vuruvayi began, glancing around at each of his friends. "But I don't want us to be like every other criminal crew out there. We're not just out to get rich—we're out to make an impact. And if we're going to do that, we need a code. Something that guides us."

Dumi raised an eyebrow, intrigued. "What do you have in mind, V?"

Vuruvayi took a deep breath. "We don't hit just anyone. We go after people and companies who deserve it—corrupt corporations, crooked politicians, those who steal from the people. This isn't about causing chaos for its own sake. We target those who are exploiting the system, profiting at the expense of everyday people."

The room was silent for a moment as the team considered this new direction. Each of them had their reasons for joining this life, but the idea of having a purpose beyond the money was something that resonated deeply.

DEFINING THE CODE

Vuruvayi continued, "We'll focus on corporations taking advantage of the poor, businesses cheating their employees, politicians who misuse public funds. But no small businesses, no individuals just trying to make a living. We only hit the ones who have exploited others, who are corrupt to the core."

Bheka nodded, a smile creeping onto his face. "I like it. It's like we're giving them a taste of their own medicine. These are the people who've been getting away with this for years. It's time someone held them accountable."

Linda leaned forward, her eyes gleaming with enthusiasm. "And we can make sure people know about it. Imagine—the money we steal from these corrupt companies goes back to the communities they've been exploiting. We could change lives."

Tumi's voice was thoughtful. "If we stick to this code, we're doing more than taking. We're rebuilding, giving back to the very people these companies overlook. We're not just criminals; we're leveling the field."

Dumi chuckled. "So, Robin Hood in 21st-century Jo'burg?"

Vuruvayi grinned. "Exactly. But we're not just giving the money away. We invest in the communities—schools, healthcare, small businesses. It's not just charity; it's real, lasting change. And it keeps us under the radar, because who's going to report us when they're benefiting?"

The idea sparked something in each of them, bringing a sense of purpose to their skills and ambitions. They weren't just in it for the thrill or the cash; they were out to reshape the city.

THE CODE IN PRACTICE

To solidify their commitment, they decided on three simple rules:

1. **Only Target the Corrupt**: Corporations and individuals who exploit, manipulate, or harm the people of South Africa.

2. **Leave No Trace**: Their heists would be precise, leaving behind no unnecessary damage or harm to innocent people.

3. **Give Back**: A portion of every score would be reinvested into the communities they came from, to uplift and build opportunities where there were none.

As they put the code in place, Vuruvayi felt a sense of clarity. This wasn't just about taking from those who had more; it was about creating a legacy of justice, however unconventional.

"From here on out," he said, his voice steady, "we're not just thieves. We're setting things right, one heist at a time. We'll make millions, but we'll also make a difference."

The others raised their glasses, each silently committing to the code and the mission it represented. From that day on, they weren't just a crew—they were a force, moving through Johannesburg like ghosts, bringing justice where none had been before.

Chapter 7: The Financial Upsurge

AS THEIR HEISTS GAINED momentum, Vuruvayi and his crew had settled into a steady rhythm, targeting corrupt corporations and politicians with each carefully crafted job. They had been cautious, spreading their funds through small investments and quiet cash flows to avoid raising suspicions. But there was only so much that small-scale investments could do for an operation as ambitious as theirs. Then came the opportunity they had been waiting for: a financial windfall that would change everything.

THE BREAKTHROUGH OPPORTUNITY

It began with Dumi, who had been carefully monitoring Johannesburg's financial networks, scanning for corporate loopholes and hidden assets ripe for the taking. One evening, he stumbled upon something significant: a mining corporation known for its shady dealings and questionable labor practices. The company had hidden away millions in offshore accounts, avoiding taxes and accumulating massive profits at the expense of its workers and surrounding communities.

"Guys, I think I found our golden ticket," Dumi announced, gathering the team around his laptop. "This mining corporation, Valta Minerals—they've been evading taxes and hiding their earnings offshore. They're sitting on millions, untouchable to authorities but accessible to the right minds."

Linda, who was ever-ready to dive into the digital side of things, leaned forward. "And let me guess—you want us to become those 'right minds'?"

Dumi nodded, grinning. "Exactly. If we can tap into these offshore accounts, it'll be enough to fund us for years. We'll be able to expand our reach, invest in serious equipment, and take our operations to a whole new level. This isn't just about stealing—it's about rewriting the game."

The Heist That Changes Everything

The plan took weeks of meticulous preparation. Linda hacked into Valta Minerals' system, mapping out its entire financial structure while ensuring her tracks were hidden at every turn. She discovered that the corporation's accounts were layered with multiple security levels, each designed to keep prying eyes out.

"I've cracked into their server room and got access to the offshore transaction histories," Linda explained one evening, a look of intense focus in her eyes. "But there's more. They've got a Swiss bank account with triple-layer encryption. This is where they're stashing the serious money, and it's not going to be easy."

Dumi worked alongside her, using his knowledge of finance to decode the complex web of transactions. After weeks of sleepless nights, double-checking every digital footprint, they were finally ready.

With Bheka orchestrating misdirection tactics and Tumi planning their logistics, the team executed their heist with clockwork precision. Linda rerouted their entry points, Dumi orchestrated the transfers, and within hours, they had siphoned off millions from Valta's hidden accounts. The corporation would be none the wiser—by the time they realized the money was missing, it would be too late.

STEPPING UP THE GAME

The financial breakthrough transformed everything. No longer constrained by tight budgets, Vuruvayi's crew could finally put their full ambitions into play. With their newfound wealth, they bought high-end surveillance gear, communication devices, getaway cars, and even secured safehouses in several locations around Johannesburg and nearby townships. They were able to hire contacts and insiders to provide them with tips on targets and up-to-date information on corporate weaknesses.

Dumi took charge of investing their wealth through channels that were untouchable, but this time, he aimed higher. Instead of small, scattered businesses, he bought stakes in larger ventures—factories, logistics companies, even a small chain of grocery stores that served underprivileged areas. Through these legitimate channels, their illicit funds were cleaned, growing under a guise of legitimate wealth that would both disguise and sustain them.

Their influence grew as well. With the added income, Vuruvayi saw the opportunity to extend their reach beyond personal gain. They funded local schools, built playgrounds, and improved infrastructure in parts of Daveyton and nearby townships, making a real difference for families who had long been overlooked by the authorities.

Tumi used a portion of their earnings to sponsor local athletes and artists, providing them with a chance to achieve their dreams. It wasn't just about the money anymore—it was about giving people a chance to escape the same circumstances they had all grown up in.

A NEW ERA OF CRIME and Charity

With more resources, the crew's operations became a seamless blend of precision and purpose. Each heist funded not only their own ambitions but also projects that uplifted the communities around them. They targeted influential politicians who had been pocketing public funds, redirecting those ill-gotten gains to rebuild schools and clinics.

Bheka, who was once purely a master of persuasion, found himself involved in community outreach projects. Using his charm, he became the public face of their charitable efforts, setting up meetings with community leaders and distributing funds under the guise of an anonymous benefactor. Through him, Vuruvayi's team gained a level of protection they hadn't anticipated; people in the communities began seeing them as heroes rather than criminals.

Their heists became known for leaving something behind—a donation to a local shelter, a new facility for a school, or job opportunities in struggling neighborhoods. People whispered about them, calling them "the Robin Hoods of Jo'burg," though they operated under an anonymity that kept their true identities safe.

A WARNING AND A REVELATION

One night, as they celebrated their latest heist—a successful raid on a corrupt investment firm that had been embezzling retirement funds—Vuruvayi raised his glass.

"This is just the beginning," he said, his eyes serious even in the midst of their celebration. "We're building something bigger than ourselves. But remember the code. We don't just take—we rebuild."

The team clinked their glasses, but Bheka, ever perceptive, noticed a hint of worry in Vuruvayi's eyes. After the others left, he lingered, pulling Vuruvayi aside.

"You're worried, aren't you?" Bheka asked.

Vuruvayi nodded. "This lifestyle—there's no blueprint for what we're doing. With every heist, we're stepping into uncharted territory. And if we slip up, even once, everything we've built could come crashing down."

Bheka placed a hand on his shoulder. "Then we just make sure we don't slip. We've got each other. We're more than just criminals, V—we're family. And no matter how high we climb, we do it together."

With their fortunes secure, their code set, and their ambitions soaring, Vuruvayi's crew moved forward into a new era of their criminal empire. They had the resources, the skills, and the purpose. And with every heist, they weren't just enriching themselves—they were rewriting the rules for the entire city, one job at a time.

Part 2: Reign of Terror in Johannesburg

Chapter 8: The Perfect Heist

THE CITY OF JOHANNESBURG, known for its towering skyline and bustling energy, felt different that week. Rumors had spread of an ambitious bank robbery underway—a heist so audacious it seemed impossible. But for Vuruvayi and his crew, this wasn't just a test of their skills; it was their chance to prove themselves at an entirely new level.

After months of meticulous planning, they were ready. Their target was the Diamond City Bank, one of the most secure financial institutions in the country and a notorious supporter of corrupt dealings. The vault within held enough wealth to sustain the team's ambitions for years. But more importantly, the job's precision would establish them as legends.

PREPPING FOR THE HEIST

The heist required every member to operate at their peak. In their usual hideout, Vuruvayi laid out the plan in vivid detail.

"Diamond City Bank has security systems on par with Fort Knox. It's layered with motion sensors, infrared cameras, biometric locks, and rotating guards. If we're going to do this, every one of us needs to execute perfectly. There's no room for error," Vuruvayi explained, his voice calm but intense.

He looked at Linda. "You'll handle the cyber security systems. We'll need access to their surveillance feeds and control over their alarms. Can you do it?"

Linda nodded confidently. "I've been studying their firewall for weeks. They have some advanced countermeasures, but they're nothing I haven't handled before."

Vuruvayi turned to Dumi. "You're our finance guy. We need clean transfers without raising flags."

Dumi smiled. "I'll set up shell accounts for the funds. By the time they notice the money's gone, we'll have it spread out and hidden."

Tumi and Bheka exchanged a glance, ready for their roles in logistics and psychology. They would be the ones to manage distractions, create alibis, and handle the physical aspects of the operation.

"Let's make history," Vuruvayi said, sealing their commitment.

※

EXECUTION: THE DAY of the Heist

The night of the heist, each of them was in place, their roles unfolding with flawless precision.

Linda: The Cyber Wizard

In an unmarked van across the street, Linda was surrounded by monitors, her fingers flying over the keyboard as she hacked into the bank's surveillance system. Within seconds, she had looped the cameras, making it appear as if the bank was empty and inactive.

"Cameras are down, and the alarms are on a 15-minute delay. If anyone checks, they'll see everything is normal," Linda reported, her voice steady.

Bheka: The Master of Distraction

While Linda worked on security, Bheka was at the front of the bank, posing as a delivery driver. He caused just enough commotion to draw attention from the guards, his charm diverting them while he subtly placed a small device near the entry gate—an electromagnetic blocker that would disable external signals temporarily.

"Gentlemen, I appreciate your patience. Just a little paperwork, and I'll be out of your way," he said with a friendly smile as the guards glanced at each other, already feeling the pull of his charisma.

Dumi: The Financial Mastermind

Inside the vault room, Dumi worked quickly, using a cloned employee ID card Linda had obtained. He swiped it across the vault's biometric scanner, giving them temporary access. Then, using his knowledge of finance, he initiated transfers to multiple shell accounts, each carefully coded to prevent tracking.

"It's going smoothly," he whispered. "Funds are dispersing. The bank won't even know the cash is gone until they run their end-of-day checks."

Tumi: The Logistics Expert

Tumi handled the physical side of the operation with ease, carrying in empty bags that would soon be filled with cash. His role was to move quickly and quietly, ensuring that they left no physical trace behind. He moved with practiced precision, organizing the loot as Dumi completed each transfer.

With everything in place, Tumi reported, "Loot is secured. Time to make our way out."

Vuruvayi: The Leader

As the others worked, Vuruvayi remained vigilant, coordinating the team's efforts and watching the clock. Every second mattered. He oversaw every detail, ensuring no one deviated from the plan. He had calculated their exit routes, timing them to slip away just as the guards' attention was drawn back to their posts.

When each step was complete, Vuruvayi gave the signal. "It's time. Everyone move."

THE GREAT ESCAPE

With their haul secured and all digital trails wiped, the team exited as smoothly as they had entered. Bheka's electromagnetic blocker deactivated as he left, restoring all communications. The guards remained oblivious, returning to their rounds without realizing they had just witnessed the most flawless heist in Johannesburg's history.

Linda shut down her computer, re-encrypting all access points she had breached. Dumi completed the last of the financial transfers, leaving behind only ghost accounts that would dissipate within hours. And Tumi loaded the loot into their vehicle, preparing for a seamless escape route.

The entire heist had taken under thirty minutes. In and out with no alarms, no security breaches, and no sign of entry. It was a job so perfect that the bank wouldn't notice anything until it was far too late.

CELEBRATING THE VICTORY

As they regrouped later that night, adrenaline was still running high. The sense of accomplishment was overwhelming; they had just pulled off a heist so sophisticated that no one would ever believe it could have been executed by a small crew of young, ambitious thieves from Daveyton.

Vuruvayi raised his glass in a quiet toast. "To us—the team that makes the impossible look easy. Tonight, we've set the bar, not just for ourselves but for everyone who thinks they own this city. Johannesburg is ours."

They clinked their glasses, each member smiling with a mixture of pride and awe. They had done it. They had pulled off the perfect heist, making millions without a trace.

THE FALLOUT

The next day, Johannesburg buzzed with disbelief as news broke of the Diamond City Bank's inexplicable loss. Forensic analysts scoured the vault, the records, the accounts—finding nothing. No forced entry, no signs of hacking, and no trail of missing funds. It was a mystery that left authorities baffled and the bank humiliated.

Meanwhile, Vuruvayi and his crew continued with their everyday lives, their newly acquired wealth tucked safely within their ever-growing network of shell corporations and hidden investments. To the outside world, they were anonymous, ordinary citizens. But they knew they had ascended to a new level of infamy, one that solidified their place as Johannesburg's greatest—and most untouchable—thieves.

For Vuruvayi, this heist marked the beginning of their reign over the city. He knew they had become something far greater than just criminals; they were myth-makers, rewriting the rules with every job. And as he looked out over the city, he felt the thrill of what was to come, knowing that they were only just beginning.

Chapter 9: The Electronic Takeover

JOHANNESBURG'S STREETS were alive, as usual, with the hum of traffic, blinking streetlights, and crowds moving under the all-seeing eyes of the city's surveillance cameras. But tonight, as Vuruvayi's crew prepared for their most ambitious job yet, those eyes would be blind.

Linda, the team's tech mastermind, sat hunched over her setup, deep in concentration. For weeks, she'd been studying Johannesburg's entire surveillance network, deciphering every line of code, every access point, every vulnerability. Her mission tonight was clear: to hack into the city's surveillance systems and effectively "turn off" the police's eyes and ears, granting the crew a window of total invisibility.

THE SETUP

"This isn't just any job," Linda said, addressing the crew from her makeshift command center. "Johannesburg's surveillance system is linked to every major intersection, government building, and bank in the city. And it's monitored by one of the most secure agencies we've faced so far."

Vuruvayi nodded, his face a mask of focused intensity. "And can you pull it off?"

Linda gave a small, confident smile. "Not only can I pull it off, but they won't even know they've been hacked until it's too late. I'll redirect their feeds to pre-recorded footage that loops seamlessly. For tonight, it'll look like the city is perfectly quiet."

Bheka whistled in admiration. "Girl, you're about to pull off the ultimate ghosting."

THE HACK BEGINS

As the others prepared for their roles in the operation, Linda got to work. With her fingers flying over the keyboard, she bypassed layers of encryption, each one more complex than the last. To the average eye, the surveillance feed seemed impenetrable, but Linda saw the vulnerabilities others missed. Her focus was absolute, her mind moving at lightning speed as she navigated the city's digital infrastructure.

Once she was inside, Linda mapped out the critical zones: the police headquarters, major intersections, and key checkpoints. With a few keystrokes, she injected a program that would feed the surveillance system a steady loop of inactive, mundane scenes. To anyone monitoring, it would look like nothing was happening across Johannesburg. No suspicious vehicles, no masked figures. Just the everyday rhythm of the city.

"Surveillance is looped," Linda announced over her headset. "We're invisible."

BLINDING THE POLICE

At the Johannesburg Police Department, the night-shift officers sat at their consoles, monitoring rows of screens showing the city's surveillance footage. Unaware of Linda's intrusion, they watched as traffic lights changed, cars rolled by, and people went about their business. But what they didn't know was that every frame they saw was carefully curated by Linda's looping program.

For an added layer of security, she rerouted all police dispatch communications through a secondary server, delaying response times and diverting calls across different precincts. Any calls made to report suspicious activity near their target would be lost in a tangle of redirected connections.

Inside their van, the crew prepared to move. Vuruvayi glanced at Linda, who was perched with headphones on, her eyes glued to her monitors.

"Everything good?" he asked.

"Smooth as silk," she replied. "As far as the police are concerned, we don't exist tonight."

EXECUTING THE JOB

The crew moved with the precision of a well-oiled machine, confident in their invisibility. With Bheka on lookout, they entered their target building—a high-profile government building known to hold valuable financial records they intended to expose. Their mission was twofold: to make their mark on the corrupt elite and to send a message that they were untouchable.

With Linda's digital takeover, they moved from room to room, collecting the files they needed, knowing there wasn't a single camera to catch their movements. Every time they passed a security camera, it was blind, playing back footage of empty corridors.

Meanwhile, Linda kept an eye on her monitors, tracking police radio channels to ensure they were unaware. As a final precaution, she looped any CCTV footage surrounding their getaway routes, leaving nothing for anyone to trace.

"We're clear," Linda reported after they exited the building. "Not a single trace left behind."

LEAVING THE POLICE Baffled

By the time the authorities realized something had happened, Vuruvayi and his team were long gone, their getaway vehicle safely tucked away and every piece of incriminating evidence erased. When the police finally tried to review the surveillance footage, all they found was hours of empty corridors and silent intersections.

The city was in an uproar the following morning, as news spread of the daring heist on a high-security government building with not a single camera recording any suspicious movement. The police were left scratching their heads, baffled by the seamless precision with which the crew had carried out their mission.

In their hideout, Linda reveled in the success of her hack, her heart still pounding from the adrenaline. For the first time, they hadn't just escaped detection—they'd rendered the entire police force powerless, leaving them blind and clueless in the wake of their crime.

Celebrating the Triumph

As they celebrated that night, Vuruvayi raised a toast to Linda. "To the tech wizard who made it all happen," he said with a grin. "Tonight, we took over an entire city, and no one even knew it."

Linda chuckled, her eyes gleaming with pride. "This is just the beginning. Now that we've cracked the city's surveillance, we can own every corner of Johannesburg whenever we need."

From that night on, the police department and security firms across Johannesburg were on edge, knowing that somewhere in the shadows lurked a ghostly presence that could manipulate the entire city's eyes and ears. For Vuruvayi and his crew, it was a new era—their reign over Johannesburg had officially begun, and the city would never see them coming.

Chapter 10: Influencing the Influencers

VURUVAYI AND HIS CREW had risen to a level where stealing money alone wasn't enough. Now, they wanted power—true power over Johannesburg's elite. It was time to move beyond simple heists. They needed people in high places to pull strings, overlook certain activities, and feed them valuable information. For this, they set their sights on manipulating influential people across the city, forming a web of corrupted allies that could work in their favor.

They met in their hideout, and Vuruvayi laid out the new plan, the outline of a strategy that went far beyond their previous jobs.

"We have the money, and we have the skills," Vuruvayi began, his gaze moving over each member of the team. "Now, we need leverage. Politicians, business moguls, police commissioners—we need people like them under our influence. We're building something bigger than ourselves here, and we can't do it alone."

FINDING THE TARGETS

THE FIRST STEP WAS identifying people who held influence and sway over Johannesburg's institutions. Tumi, with his expertise in logistics and planning, mapped out an intricate network of key players in various fields—media moguls, local politicians, high-ranking police officials, and prominent businesspeople. He researched their connections, vices, and vulnerabilities, noting anyone who seemed susceptible to persuasion, blackmail, or bribery.

"Some of these people already operate in the gray area," Tumi reported. "They have skeletons they want to keep buried. And for those who don't, well, we can create them."

Building Connections

Linda and Bheka took the lead in approaching their targets. Linda, with her digital prowess, was able to dig up incriminating information, from shady financial deals to personal indiscretions. Meanwhile, Bheka, with his charm and persuasion skills, was the perfect frontman. He carefully orchestrated chance encounters at exclusive events, fundraisers, and high-end clubs, drawing these influential figures into their web one by one.

Their first target was Councillor Nkosi, a rising politician with ambitions to run for mayor. Linda had uncovered evidence of illicit payments made to Nkosi by local developers in exchange for prime land deals. Vuruvayi crafted a clever message to Nkosi, hinting at knowledge of these dealings and offering him a simple choice: work with them, or face exposure.

"I don't need any trouble," Nkosi replied, nervously, when he met Bheka to discuss the arrangement. "What do you need from me?"

"A simple exchange of favors," Bheka assured him with a calm smile. "Whenever we need certain issues overlooked, we trust you'll handle it. In return, you have our protection—and, if necessary, our silence."

Strategic Partnerships

One by one, they built their network, each new ally bringing a different advantage. There was Dr. Pillay, a prominent health official who was eager to fund her private research and gladly accepted "donations" in exchange for medical favors and insider information on hospital contracts. Then came Thabo Masondo, the CEO of a major security firm, who provided access to high-grade equipment and occasionally "missed" alerts from his own systems when needed.

The media, too, was a key component of their influence strategy. Vuruvayi knew that public perception was crucial; they needed both to appear invisible when required and powerful when advantageous. Linda hacked into the email accounts of a few prominent journalists, gaining access to private information that could be used as leverage. Once inside, they could control which stories surfaced—and which didn't. In exchange, they offered select journalists exclusive "insider" tips and stories, carefully managed to suit the crew's agenda.

THE WEB TIGHTENS

Within months, Vuruvayi's crew had woven a web of power that stretched across Johannesburg. At a mere phone call, they could request favors, delay police action, or sway public opinion. And because every ally was bound by self-interest, fear, or greed, loyalty was guaranteed.

There were occasional challenges—some influential figures resisted or doubted their intentions. For those, the team used subtle intimidation tactics. A note slipped into a personal bag, a private recording left on their voicemail, a photo of an indiscretion on their phone. Each reminder was tailored to the target's specific fears, reinforcing the message: cooperate, and everyone benefits.

TURNING THE TABLES

With their network established, Vuruvayi's team was no longer merely a group of criminals. They were becoming an invisible influence over the city itself. For Vuruvayi, this was the beginning of true power. Now, they could not only evade the law but also steer it to their advantage. If they needed to make a move without interference, they simply had to make a few calls. If they wanted to stir up trouble for a competitor, they could prompt a story leak or a quiet investigation. The city was now, in effect, under their influence.

A TOAST TO POWER

Back in their hideout one evening, Vuruvayi and his crew reflected on their recent successes. They raised their glasses, each toasting to the web of influence they had built.

"To our friends in high places," Vuruvayi said, a smirk crossing his face. "Tonight, Johannesburg bends to our will."

The team clinked glasses, aware that they had reached a new level in their journey. They had become more than just a group of skilled criminals. They were puppet masters, pulling strings behind the scenes, each move strengthening their hold over Johannesburg. And with their network of corrupted allies, they knew there were no limits to what they could achieve.

Chapter 11: Money Talks

THE TEAM'S HEISTS AND newfound connections had made them wealthy beyond their wildest dreams, and now, Vuruvayi knew it was time to wield that wealth with purpose. It was no longer just about evading the law; it was about ensuring they held power over it. To do that, they needed the right people in their pocket—and they knew that, in Johannesburg, money could talk louder than any threat.

Identifying Key Players

Around a dimly lit table, Tumi had laid out an extensive list of officials who were crucial to their long-term protection. "These are the people we need," he explained, tapping his finger on the names of police officers, district attorneys, judges, and influential city clerks. "They control evidence, authorize investigations, and can make or break any case that gets too close to us."

"Perfect," Vuruvayi replied. "If they value their careers—and their bank accounts—then they'll do as we say."

The Strategy: A Web of Bribes

Each bribe was carefully planned and tailored to the person receiving it. Bheka, with his charm and experience in persuasion, was assigned to make the initial contacts. He approached each target with a carefully curated offer, ensuring the bribe didn't feel like a threat but rather a mutually beneficial arrangement. The key was subtlety: no large sums upfront, only enough to catch their attention and leave them wanting more.

They started with Officer Maseko, a senior detective notorious for being "flexible" when it came to bending the rules. Bheka met him over a casual drink, slipping a generous envelope under the table.

"We understand that you're responsible for overseeing some of the higher-level investigations," Bheka said smoothly. "We'd like to ensure that any cases involving our... associates... are given the appropriate attention. And by that, we mean none at all."

Maseko hesitated only for a moment before taking the envelope. He glanced at the money and smirked. "I think we can work something out."

Widening the Circle

With Maseko on board, they continued to spread their influence. Linda worked her tech magic to collect "insights" on each target, knowing exactly who had debts to pay, who had ambitions for a promotion, and who was on the verge of financial ruin. They tailored each bribe to the weaknesses and desires of each individual, making the offers nearly impossible to refuse.

For Judge Khumalo, they arranged a series of quiet payments to fund his expensive tastes in art. In exchange, he would "misplace" any warrant that threatened their operations. For the head of the evidence room, they funded his daughter's university tuition, with the understanding that certain files would go missing if their names were ever involved.

Ensuring Loyalty

Vuruvayi understood that money alone wasn't enough to secure loyalty. He needed these people to feel invested in the relationship. Periodic gifts and bonuses were distributed, but so were reminders of what they had to lose. The crew would send flowers to an official's spouse, drop off an anonymous "thank you" letter at their home, or send a mysterious text reminding them of their commitment.

And for those few who dared to resist the bribes, they had other tactics. Tumi arranged "mishaps" for a few key resisters. For one official who refused their offer, he found his car mysteriously vandalized. For another, her credit score plummeted after Linda hacked into her financial accounts. These messages were rarely ignored twice.

Immunity Secured

As months passed, their reach extended deeper into Johannesburg's institutions. Any time a police officer seemed too interested in their activities, Officer Maseko would intercept the report and "adjust" the findings. When a witness came forward about a suspicious sighting, the district attorney would quietly dismiss it, citing lack of evidence. Judge Khumalo ensured that if any of their cases ever made it to court, they would be dismissed before a trial even started.

The crew's immunity wasn't just about protection—it was power. With every official who fell under their influence, they tightened their grip over Johannesburg, becoming untouchable in the city that had once tried to keep them down.

Celebrating Their Immunity

One evening, the team gathered in their hidden lair to celebrate their recent triumphs. Their accounts were full, and their network of influence was stronger than ever. Vuruvayi raised a glass, pride shining in his eyes.

"We've built something unbreakable," he said, his voice full of conviction. "As long as money talks, we'll never fall. To a future where we answer to no one."

They toasted, each of them feeling the power of their empire, knowing they were no longer just criminals—they were untouchable architects of Johannesburg's underworld. And with every official, judge, and officer on their payroll, Vuruvayi and his team knew that no one would ever come close to stopping them.

Chapter 12: The Johannesburg Lockdown

VURUVAYI AND HIS CREW had taken Johannesburg by storm, their influence reaching every corner of the city. But as whispers of their exploits grew louder, the public began to demand action, pressuring the police force into launching a full-scale crackdown. Determined to restore their control over the city, the police commissioner announced a citywide operation targeting organized crime, with a promise to root out every syndicate, gang, and shadowy figure causing chaos in Johannesburg.

Vuruvayi knew they were the prime target.

The First Wave of the Crackdown

The initial days were intense. Police checkpoints appeared overnight, with officers stationed at key intersections and strategic locations throughout the city. Patrols increased tenfold, and raids swept through known hideouts, leaving no stone unturned. Rumors circulated that top officials were interrogating even the most minor informants, hoping for a shred of evidence that could lead them to Vuruvayi's crew.

Inside their hideout, Vuruvayi gathered the team. The usual calm that colored their planning sessions had been replaced by a tense focus. Tumi spread out a map on the table, marking each location where police activity had surged.

"They're hitting the streets hard," Tumi reported, his face taut with concern. "Every contact I've spoken to says they're cracking down on any operation that even remotely resembles ours."

"Let them try," Vuruvayi replied, his voice steady. "They're playing checkers, while we're playing chess. We just need to stay ahead of them."

Staying One Step Ahead

Linda, the tech genius, immediately took action. She set up a live feed of police radio frequencies, decoding their communications to gain insight into upcoming raids and high-priority targets. With her network of surveillance hacks, she kept tabs on police movement across Johannesburg, ensuring that the team would be alerted to any approaching danger.

"Linda, we're counting on you to keep us invisible," Vuruvayi told her, glancing at her computer setup. "Anything suspicious, we need to know before they even think of moving."

Bheka, meanwhile, leveraged his network of allies in law enforcement. He arranged for discreet updates from officers they had on the payroll, who quietly tipped him off about internal meetings, planned checkpoints, and even the commissioner's intentions. With their influence over these officials, they managed to gain crucial insights into the police's strategy, giving them a valuable edge.

"Seems the commissioner's got a personal vendetta now," Bheka said with a smirk. "But all his moves are coming straight to us."

Evading the Raids

Despite the police's best efforts, every raid intended to corner Vuruvayi's crew turned up empty. The team had perfected their system of staying mobile, changing hideouts regularly, and keeping their true headquarters hidden from even their most trusted allies. Linda monitored real-time surveillance and kept track of every raid location, and Tumi ensured they always had a secure place to regroup.

One night, as police surrounded a suspected hideout on the outskirts of Johannesburg, Vuruvayi and his team watched the raid unfold from a distance. They'd left just an hour earlier, tipped off by one of Bheka's contacts. Vuruvayi chuckled as he saw the commissioner himself overseeing the operation, his face growing more frustrated with each passing moment.

"Let them waste their time," Vuruvayi muttered. "The more they focus on dead ends, the less they can focus on us."

Diversion Tactics

As the police grew more desperate, Vuruvayi's team decided to divert attention. They staged a series of petty crimes, each one orchestrated to resemble their usual high-stakes heists but designed to leave obvious trails that pointed to unrelated gangs around the city. Linda planted false evidence in police databases, sending investigators down rabbit holes while Tumi orchestrated fake "tip-offs" to local authorities.

"Every minute they waste on a decoy is another minute we can move freely," Tumi said, explaining the diversion tactics to the team.

The strategy worked. Police resources were stretched thin as they chased down false leads, turning their focus on minor players who had nothing to do with Vuruvayi's organization. Meanwhile, the crew went about their business, unaffected by the heightened police presence.

Turning the Tables

With their diversions buying them time, Vuruvayi decided to send a message to the commissioner. He wanted the city to know that his crew was not only untouchable but also fully in control. They planned a daring heist in broad daylight, right under the commissioner's nose.

The target was a vault in the city's wealthiest district, known for its high-profile clients. On the day of the heist, Linda hacked into the building's surveillance system, looping the feeds to show empty hallways, while Bheka and Tumi slipped inside undetected. Within minutes, they secured the vault's cash and left without a trace.

The message was clear: Vuruvayi's crew was unbreakable, even in the face of Johannesburg's "lockdown."

The next morning, news of the heist dominated every headline, and the commissioner faced fierce criticism. It was one thing to announce a crackdown on organized crime, but it was another to let the city's most infamous crew walk away with millions. The public began to lose faith in the police's ability to contain the syndicates operating within Johannesburg.

A New Era of Control

With every move the police made, Vuruvayi and his team stayed a step ahead, outsmarting each new tactic with precision and foresight. In response to the "lockdown," they solidified their power in ways that no crackdown could undo. They continued to build their web of influence, bribing more officials, expanding their alliances, and ensuring that every key player within the city owed them a favor.

And as they watched the police commissioner struggle to regain control, Vuruvayi's crew knew they had won.

In their hideout, Vuruvayi looked around at his team, each one smiling with satisfaction at the chaos they'd managed to elude. "They tried to take us down," he said, his voice filled with pride, "but we showed them who really runs this city."

The Johannesburg lockdown had ended not with their capture, but with their victory. In the wake of the crackdown, Vuruvayi and his team emerged stronger, their control over the city tighter than ever. They'd outsmarted the police, outmaneuvered the government, and reminded everyone that in Johannesburg, they were untouchable.

Chapter 13: Community Investment Begins

VURUVAYI STOOD AT THE heart of Daveyton, looking over the dusty, bustling neighborhood he'd once called home. It was a place he knew intimately—the winding streets, the makeshift shacks, the children running barefoot. The memories of his own difficult upbringing flooded back, filling him with a resolve that fueled his ambitions. He turned to his team, a thoughtful expression crossing his face.

"It's time we give back," he said, gesturing at the scene before them. "This city has its flaws, but it's our city. We're going to make it better."

The team had grown wealthy, powerful, and untouchable, but now they needed a legitimate image. Vuruvayi's plan was to invest in community projects across Johannesburg, not only as a cover for their activities but also as a genuine step toward uplifting the communities that had shaped them. By investing in the people, they would earn both loyalty and protection from those who could benefit from their success.

The First Project: A Community Center

The first project was a community center in Daveyton, a place where the youth could gather safely, find educational resources, and learn new skills. The official announcement was made with modest fanfare, Vuruvayi keeping a low profile as a "private donor" behind the initiative. They put Tumi in charge of the logistics, and he worked closely with local contractors to ensure the center was built quickly and efficiently.

As the community center began to take shape, word spread through the township. Children gathered to watch the construction, while parents asked questions about the programs the center would offer. The mood in Daveyton shifted from skepticism to excitement as residents saw tangible proof of the project's benefits.

"This is for them," Vuruvayi told his crew during one of their meetings. "They've suffered enough without access to resources. We're changing that."

Expanding Their Influence

With the success of the community center, Vuruvayi's team quickly expanded their projects across Johannesburg. In Soweto, they funded a skills development workshop where locals could learn carpentry, welding, and other trades. In Alexandra, they set up a computer lab, allowing young people to learn about technology and coding. Every project was tailored to meet the specific needs of each community, showing that Vuruvayi's crew understood and cared for the people they were helping.

Linda managed the digital campaign for these projects, making sure their work was seen by as many people as possible. Photos of smiling children, young adults learning new skills, and families benefiting from free resources filled social media feeds. People began to see Vuruvayi's crew as heroes, a group with the power to change lives rather than the feared criminals they had once been.

Winning Over the Community

Bheka's charm came in handy as he attended community events, mingling with locals and establishing connections with influential leaders. He spoke at the launch of each project, giving speeches that resonated with the residents' struggles and aspirations.

"Every child deserves a chance to dream," he said at the opening of the skills development center. "We're here to ensure they have the tools to turn those dreams into reality."

As the projects multiplied, so did their popularity. In townships and neighborhoods once plagued by neglect, Vuruvayi's crew was now viewed as champions of the people. They provided scholarships, offered free health clinics, and sponsored sports events. They did all of this without ever revealing the wealth's origin, presenting themselves simply as people determined to uplift their communities.

A Shield of Loyalty

The impact of their investments went beyond goodwill. The residents, grateful for the opportunities and improvements, began to view Vuruvayi's team as one of their own. As a result, the community started to protect them. When outsiders asked questions about suspicious activities, locals turned them away or deflected with stories of the positive impact Vuruvayi's team had made.

Police officers, even those unaffiliated with the crew, found it difficult to pursue investigations in areas where Vuruvayi's influence ran deep. They were met with resistance and silence from people who refused to betray the figures who had given so much to their neighborhoods.

"We've created a fortress of loyalty," Tumi observed one day, marveling at how the people they'd once hidden from now stood ready to defend them.

Genuine Transformation

For Vuruvayi, what had begun as a clever cover to protect their activities started to feel like something more profound. He saw lives genuinely changing, young people escaping poverty, and families feeling a renewed sense of pride in their communities. This transformation wasn't just for appearances—it became a core part of the crew's purpose. The team felt an unexpected satisfaction from seeing the tangible results of their projects, and it reinforced their commitment to continue building up the communities they had once watched struggle.

One evening, as they looked out over the completed community center, Vuruvayi turned to his friends.

"We've done something good here," he said, his voice laced with pride. "Maybe it doesn't erase the things we've done, but it's a start."

The crew nodded in agreement, each of them silently reflecting on the power they now wielded—not just over Johannesburg's criminal underworld, but over the hearts and minds of its people.

Chapter 14: Public Robin Hoods

THE COMMUNITY INVESTMENTS had taken on a life of their own. New parks, youth centers, and educational initiatives popped up around Johannesburg, each one funded by Vuruvayi and his crew. They worked discreetly, presenting themselves only as benefactors, yet the people they helped spoke of them in near-mythical terms. These men had come from nowhere, it seemed, bringing resources and hope to communities that had long been neglected.

It wasn't long before the media took notice.

A Stir in the Newsrooms

Journalists initially dismissed the rumors of anonymous benefactors pouring money into Johannesburg's townships. But as they investigated, the stories were impossible to ignore. Reports started surfacing of a new community center in Soweto, a tech lab in Alexandra, free clinics in Tembisa, and scholarship funds appearing out of thin air in neighborhoods that desperately needed them. Articles speculated on who these mysterious benefactors were, their source of funds, and why they were so committed to uplifting these areas.

One article stood out among the rest, capturing public attention with a bold headline: *"Modern-Day Robin Hoods Transforming Johannesburg's Forgotten Communities."*

The piece detailed the scope of the crew's projects, describing how they seemed to "appear out of the blue, fixing what the government had left undone." It painted Vuruvayi and his team as local legends, their faces unknown but their presence undeniable. The article struck a chord with readers, and soon other media outlets picked up the story.

The Birth of the Legend

Once the story spread, the public embraced it. People began calling Vuruvayi's crew "Johannesburg's Robin Hoods," a title that stuck. Community members, protective of the benefactors' anonymity, spun tales of shadowy figures who worked under the cover of night, restoring hope to the townships. Stories of these "Robin Hoods" circulated on social media, where images of newly built parks, schools, and clinics were shared alongside the legend.

The coverage drew the attention of people across South Africa, many of whom resonated with the story of underprivileged communities finally receiving the resources they deserved. Vuruvayi's crew became icons, symbols of defiance against a system that had long overlooked them. Even people in positions of power began speaking about the "mystery philanthropists" with a sense of reluctant admiration.

The Crew's Reaction

Inside their hidden lair, the crew watched as their reputation transformed. Tumi scrolled through social media, laughing as he read post after post speculating on the identity of the Robin Hoods of Johannesburg.

"They think we're heroes!" he said, shaking his head in disbelief.

Bheka grinned. "Who knew crime could get you this kind of respect?"

Linda leaned back in her chair, smirking as she flipped through the latest newspaper articles. "It's genius, really. This cover might be the best thing we've ever done. Nobody would suspect a bunch of 'public heroes' to be running the city's biggest syndicate."

For Vuruvayi, the public adoration was both exhilarating and sobering. He hadn't set out to become a symbol; he'd just wanted to protect his crew and give back to the community. Yet seeing how their actions resonated with the people reminded him of the impact they could have, and he found himself embracing this unexpected role.

"We've built more than just a criminal empire," Vuruvayi said quietly. "We've built a legacy. People are looking to us now, relying on us. It's... humbling."

Complications of Fame

The public support was a double-edged sword, though. The media attention, while reinforcing their image, had also caught the eye of those eager to investigate further. The police, previously thwarted at every turn, couldn't ignore the whispers that Johannesburg's "Robin Hoods" might be more than mere philanthropists. Suspicion grew, and pressure mounted on law enforcement to "unmask" these benefactors.

Detective Sizwe Nkomo, a veteran officer with a reputation for tenacity, took it upon himself to unravel the mystery. He had a hunch that these Robin Hoods were hiding something more sinister, and he was determined to uncover it.

Nkomo read every article, watched every news segment, and pieced together every known detail of the mysterious crew. He became a frequent presence in the communities where Vuruvayi's team had invested, questioning locals, digging for information, and even offering rewards for anyone willing to speak up. But each time, he encountered the same loyalty that Vuruvayi had built—a wall of silence.

The Power of Loyalty

The community's unwavering support became an impenetrable shield. Residents refused to cooperate with Nkomo, viewing him as an outsider trying to dismantle something positive. They told him stories of the incredible transformations happening around them, from new schools and medical clinics to scholarships and job training programs. But when he pressed them for specifics, names, or descriptions, they would only shake their heads.

"No one would betray those who saved us," a local elder told Nkomo when he came around one evening. "Our children have futures because of them. We won't speak ill of them."

Despite Nkomo's best efforts, the Robin Hood myth only strengthened. Vuruvayi and his crew had become untouchable not because of bribes or fear, but because they had won the hearts of the people.

Embracing the Role

As weeks passed, the crew grew accustomed to their new roles as the people's champions. Vuruvayi continued their projects, setting up food banks and even hosting community events where scholarships and grants were awarded under their mysterious foundation. The crew appeared more public than ever, but still, no one outside their circle knew their true identities.

They weren't simply criminals hiding behind a philanthropic front—they were men who had risen from hardship and now wielded their power to defy a broken system. For Vuruvayi, this was no longer just about outsmarting the police or keeping his crew safe. It was about building a legacy that would live on.

And as long as Johannesburg believed in its Robin Hoods, Vuruvayi and his team were safe—protected by the loyalty of a city they had managed to captivate.

Chapter 15: The Biggest Score Yet

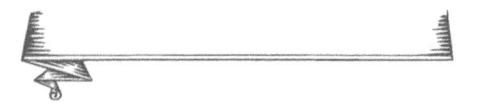

THE DIM GLOW OF CITY lights filtered through the windows of the abandoned warehouse where Vuruvayi's crew gathered, each of them a mixture of anticipation and steady resolve. They were about to embark on their biggest mission yet—a heist unlike anything they had ever attempted, one that promised the highest reward yet but carried enormous risk.

Vuruvayi scanned the faces of his friends: Linda, their tech genius, with her laptop balanced on her knee, her fingers flying over the keyboard; Bheka, the master of manipulation, cool and collected as always; Tumi, the logistics whiz, studying their floor plans for the hundredth time; and Kabelo, their finance expert, who had meticulously calculated every step of the plan. Together, they were unstoppable.

"Tonight, we'll hit the Dlamini Financial Vault," Vuruvayi announced, his voice calm and steady. "It's risky, but if we pull this off, we'll be set for life. This is the score that will cement our reputation across Johannesburg."

The Setup

The Dlamini Financial Vault wasn't just any target; it was the financial nerve center of one of the wealthiest—and most corrupt—business conglomerates in South Africa. It was rumored that the vault held millions in untraceable cash, tucked away by politicians, CEOs, and criminal organizations alike. The place was a fortress:

armed guards, state-of-the-art surveillance, and security protocols that changed by the hour.

Linda had spent weeks hacking into their system, watching their patterns, and studying the building's infrastructure. She now had temporary access to the security cameras, which would give them a short window before alarms triggered.

"We'll have fifteen minutes once we're in," Linda explained, "before the system notices the breach. We're in, grab the cash, and out. No room for mistakes."

Tumi nodded, his logistics mapped to the second. "I've calculated every possible route to avoid the guards and slip out undetected. The getaway vehicle will be waiting by the back entrance, hidden in the loading bay."

Kabelo added, "Once we're out, the funds will be laundered through multiple shell companies and funneled into our accounts under different aliases. By the time they even realize what's missing, we'll be ghosts."

The Execution

Under the cover of night, Vuruvayi and his team approached the towering building in a discreet, nondescript van. They parked in a shadowed alley near a service entrance, slipping inside just as Linda temporarily disabled the security feed. The building was silent, humming with the low murmur of machines and the distant footsteps of security guards on their rounds.

Once inside, Linda took charge, guiding the team through the maze-like corridors. "Take a left, then through the maintenance door. Two guards coming up in ten seconds—wait until they pass, then go."

They moved with precision, barely a whisper as they advanced, avoiding the cameras Linda had momentarily disabled. Every step had been rehearsed, every turn memorized.

Finally, they reached the vault. Tumi's toolkit appeared in his hands as he set to work on the lock, quickly bypassing the electronic mechanisms Linda had decoded beforehand. Within seconds, the heavy door clicked open, revealing stacks upon stacks of cash inside the secured room.

"Let's move," Vuruvayi whispered, and the team swept in, filling duffel bags with stacks of bills. The cash was packed so tightly that every bag felt like it was made of bricks. Vuruvayi's heart pounded as he looked around the vault, knowing they were securing the future they had all dreamed of.

The Getaway

Just as the last bag was zipped shut, Linda's voice crackled in their earpieces. "You've got two minutes until the system reboot. Exit now."

Without a second to waste, they sprinted back through the labyrinthine halls, moving in perfect sync. Tumi led the way, following his mapped route precisely. The guards, oblivious to the intrusion, continued their rounds as the crew slipped past them unnoticed.

They reached the loading bay, where their getaway vehicle awaited, hidden from view. As they piled in, the weight of the bags was palpable, their haul solid and real.

Linda slammed the door shut, and Tumi hit the gas. The vehicle roared to life, tearing out of the loading bay and merging seamlessly with the city traffic. They navigated the streets with practiced ease, every turn taking them further from the scene of the crime.

Behind them, alarms blared as the vault's security system reactivated, but by then, they were blocks away, disappearing into the depths of Johannesburg's midnight streets.

The Aftermath

Back at their hideout, the crew unpacked their haul. The stacks of cash were endless, the room filling with an overwhelming sense of accomplishment and disbelief. They'd pulled off the impossible, robbing one of the most secure vaults in the country and emerging with millions.

Vuruvayi grinned as he looked at his friends, who were equally exhausted and elated. "We did it," he said, his voice filled with pride. "Tonight, we became legends."

The success of the heist echoed through Johannesburg's criminal circles and beyond. Word spread fast—no one had ever dared hit Dlamini Financial, let alone gotten away with it. Vuruvayi's crew had pulled off a heist so daring, so perfectly executed, that they became untouchable legends in the underworld.

The media reported on the heist with shock and awe, headlines proclaiming the audacity of the unknown group who had struck at the heart of Johannesburg's wealthiest. Speculations ran wild, theories floated, and every known criminal outfit tried to claim responsibility—but everyone knew only one crew could pull off a heist of this magnitude.

The Robin Hoods of Johannesburg had once again struck, their reputation as the city's most elusive and unstoppable masterminds now cemented.

A New Dawn

With millions more in their coffers, Vuruvayi's crew expanded their operations, reinvesting in their community projects and securing allies throughout the city. They used their wealth to uplift more neighborhoods, their empire now built on both power and purpose.

As they looked ahead to their next moves, one thing was certain: Vuruvayi and his crew were untouchable, the modern-day Robin Hoods who had achieved the impossible and won the loyalty of a city. They were legends in their own time, with a future as rich as the dreams that had once driven them out of the shadows and into the spotlight.

Chapter 16: The Unbreakable Network

IN THE DIM GLOW OF their hideout, Vuruvayi studied the map of South Africa pinned to the wall, each city and township marked with potential connections. Their recent heist had granted them immense wealth and infamy, but to stay ahead of the authorities and expand their influence, they needed allies. They needed people in every city who could provide intel, move resources, and handle logistics when necessary. Their empire couldn't be limited to Johannesburg alone—it was time to spread their reach across the nation.

The idea of building a network had started as a small notion, a way to create escape routes and safehouses in case things went wrong. But Vuruvayi knew that with the right people, it could become an unbreakable chain that stretched from the townships of Soweto to the skyscrapers of Cape Town.

"We're going to build a network," Vuruvayi declared to the crew one evening. "One that reaches into every city, every township, and stays unbreakable. We'll have eyes and ears everywhere, people who can keep us informed, who believe in what we're doing."

Recruiting Begins

To recruit people, they began reaching out to trusted friends and associates in communities across South Africa. They sought people who shared a deep dissatisfaction with the government, those who felt ignored or wronged by the system. Their approach was simple yet powerful—they offered protection, resources, and purpose to those who had been overlooked by society.

Their first recruit was a taxi boss from Alexandra named Sipho, a man who controlled the routes through the sprawling township. Vuruvayi saw the potential immediately; Sipho's drivers knew every corner, every shortcut, and were experts at navigating the city without drawing attention. In exchange for funds and a promise of safety, Sipho agreed to let his fleet act as the crew's eyes and ears in Johannesburg.

Bheka worked his magic, connecting with activists, small-time hustlers, and local influencers who were loyal to their communities. He spoke of Vuruvayi's vision for a better South Africa, where their wealth was reinvested into the people. Slowly, these contacts agreed to join, becoming points of information and refuge in places where the crew would otherwise be strangers.

Linda focused on recruiting young tech-savvy students from nearby universities, training them to intercept communications, scrub data, and cover digital tracks. These recruits, scattered across different campuses, became the tech backbone of the network, allowing the crew to evade police surveillance and track their movements in real-time.

Strengthening the Connections

To strengthen loyalty, Vuruvayi ensured each new recruit felt like a vital part of the mission. They didn't see themselves as mere employees; they were part of a larger movement, one that sought to balance power and give back to the people. The crew regularly checked in with them, using encrypted channels to share plans, successes, and words of encouragement.

To maintain their loyalty, Vuruvayi made sure each member saw tangible benefits. In Soweto, they helped build a youth center where their recruits' children could study safely. In Alexandra, they funded small businesses, empowering locals to thrive. And in Cape Town, they supported a free legal clinic for disadvantaged communities, ensuring protection for those involved in their operation.

Each new addition to the network made the crew stronger, more informed, and more difficult to capture.

A New Kind of Power

With the network in place, Vuruvayi's crew could accomplish feats previously unimaginable. The police and officials were clueless to the reach of this shadowy alliance stretching across cities. When they needed to move money, their contacts in Pretoria could transfer funds across invisible channels. If an officer seemed too curious, someone in Durban would ensure they were preoccupied with a diversion.

In one case, a high-ranking detective in Johannesburg got a bit too close to identifying them. Word traveled quickly through the network, and by the time the detective arrived at their supposed location, a tip from Cape Town redirected him to a false lead.

The crew's influence was far-reaching, and people everywhere whispered about "the network" that operated outside the government's reach, offering aid and influence to communities in need.

The Next Generation

As their influence grew, Vuruvayi began identifying younger individuals with leadership potential, grooming them to take on greater roles within the network. He believed in creating a lasting legacy, a system that would function even if his crew had to step away one day. They trained these young leaders not just in logistics and planning but in the code that held their operation together—the belief that they would only ever target the corrupt and use their wealth to uplift the people.

One of their standout recruits was Thandi, a law student from Port Elizabeth. Sharp, quick-witted, and passionate about social justice, she became their legal strategist, advising them on how to navigate complex legal issues while avoiding detection. Another promising recruit, Themba, was a tech prodigy from Limpopo who showed potential as a future tech lead. Linda took him under her wing, teaching him how to control surveillance systems and encrypt data.

Rising Influence

Before long, the network had grown into something truly formidable, an empire that stretched from city to city, uniting people who had felt overlooked and powerless for years. Vuruvayi's crew became more than just criminals or Robin Hood figures—they became legends, a symbol of resistance and hope.

Their work was far from over, but with each new recruit and each expanded connection, they were building a future that could endure beyond their own lives. They had set in motion something that couldn't easily be broken, a force too large for even the most powerful to contain.

With the Unbreakable Network in place, they were no longer vulnerable to the whims of the law or the media. They were unstoppable. Vuruvayi and his crew had risen to the top, not just as criminals but as revolutionaries, reshaping South Africa from the shadows.

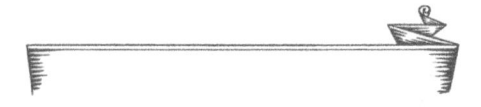

Chapter 17: Close Call

THE CREW HAD BECOME experts at staying in the shadows, their names unknown, their faces concealed from prying eyes. But for all their precautions, they knew there was always a risk—someone might stumble too close to the truth. That risk materialized one day in the form of Detective Mandla Nkomo, a veteran investigator with a nose for crime and a reputation for being relentless.

Detective Nkomo had been on the police force for two decades, witnessing the rise and fall of numerous criminal enterprises. He had watched with growing frustration as reports of Vuruvayi's crew spread, mystifying the department. There were whispers in the halls, rumors of an underground network that no one could quite grasp. The crew's heists were precise, their escapes flawless, and their impact on communities impossible to ignore. Despite the crew's Robin Hood reputation, Nkomo was determined to bring them to justice—until he found himself drawn into their world.

The Breakthrough

Late one evening, after pouring over endless reports, Nkomo noticed a pattern that others had missed. It was subtle, but enough to spark his curiosity: the heists seemed to follow a route, touching on areas that received "mysterious" donations for community projects afterward. The detective mapped out the locations, and with a shock, he realized that he could predict where the crew might strike next.

Armed with this new insight, Nkomo decided to monitor the area, hoping to catch them in the act. He knew his superiors wouldn't approve, so he kept his suspicions to himself, planning a covert stakeout. For three nights, he watched the spot, a rundown neighborhood in Johannesburg known for poverty and neglect. He was prepared for a confrontation, but what he saw on the fourth night was entirely unexpected.

Face to Face

Under the cover of darkness, Vuruvayi and his team approached an old community center. Nkomo's eyes widened as he recognized them from the descriptions: Linda, Bheka, Tumi, Kabelo, and the leader, Vuruvayi himself. He watched as they unloaded boxes filled with supplies, paint, and tools—hardly the makings of a criminal operation. He realized they weren't robbing the community; they were rebuilding it.

Suddenly, a loose piece of gravel crunched under Nkomo's foot, and all eyes turned his way. He was caught. The crew froze, their expressions hardening, prepared for a confrontation. But before anyone could react, Vuruvayi stepped forward, his gaze locked on the detective.

"You've been watching us," Vuruvayi said calmly, sizing him up. "Why?"

Nkomo considered lying, then thought better of it. "Because I know what you're doing. I know you're the ones behind the heists and the network. I don't know why you're helping the communities, but it doesn't change the fact that you're criminals."

The tension was thick, each member of the crew braced for whatever might happen next. But instead of hostility, Vuruvayi's expression softened slightly.

"Detective Nkomo," Vuruvayi began, surprising him with his knowledge, "you're right. We are criminals in the eyes of the law. But the law has left people like this community behind. We're doing what we can to give them a fighting chance."

Nkomo was silent, his mind racing. He had spent his career fighting for justice, but he knew better than anyone how flawed the system was. He had witnessed the corruption, the inequity, and the way some of his own superiors turned a blind eye to real crimes while pursuing those who had done no harm. It gnawed at him.

"You're saying the law is wrong?" Nkomo challenged, though his voice held less conviction.

"I'm saying that sometimes," Vuruvayi replied, "you have to break the law to create real justice. The kind that reaches places the government forgot."

A Crossroads

The detective wrestled with himself, torn between his duty and what he was seeing with his own eyes. But his choice became clear when Vuruvayi extended his hand.

"We don't have to be enemies, Detective. We're not here to hurt the innocent, and you've seen that. Join us. We're offering you the chance to make a difference—one that actually matters."

It was the boldest move Vuruvayi had ever made, and his crew watched, holding their breath. But in his gut, Vuruvayi had read Nkomo right. There was a part of the detective that longed for change, that was tired of seeing justice slip away.

After a long pause, Nkomo slowly reached out, grasping Vuruvayi's hand. "I won't become one of you," he said quietly, "but I'll help you where I can. I have limits. I'll be watching you, and if I ever see you crossing the line, I won't hesitate to stop you."

Vuruvayi nodded, respecting his stance. "That's all we ask, Detective. And in return, if you ever need us—if you ever need justice done, without politics or corruption—you know how to find us."

A New Ally

With Nkomo on their side, the crew's influence only grew. They had an invaluable ally in the police department, someone who could divert investigations, misdirect their pursuers, and offer insights only an insider would know. Though Nkomo maintained his distance, he became a silent partner, slipping information their way when he uncovered plans or heard chatter from superiors who were closing in on the crew.

Together, they operated in the shadows, each man understanding the other's boundaries. Nkomo never allowed himself to become a criminal, but he came to appreciate the change the crew was making. Over time, he even saw the impact of their work in the communities he once patrolled, neighborhoods that no longer looked so forgotten, places that were beginning to thrive again.

In a world where right and wrong were blurred, Vuruvayi's crew had forged an alliance with an unlikely friend, each one navigating the complex web of crime, loyalty, and justice in ways they had never anticipated. With Detective Nkomo watching their backs, they were stronger than ever, their network unbreakable and their reach expanding across South Africa.

Chapter 18: The Cape Town Expansion

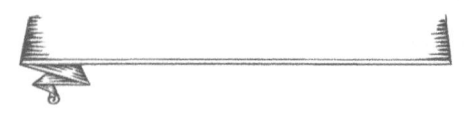

THE JOHANNESBURG OPERATIONS had cemented their power, giving them wealth, influence, and an unbreakable network in the city. But Vuruvayi knew that if they were to achieve real change and stay untouchable, their reach had to expand beyond Johannesburg. Cape Town, Durban, and Pretoria—each held unique opportunities and challenges. With Detective Nkomo feeding them intel on potential police activity and allies ready across the country, the crew set their sights on their next frontier.

Vuruvayi and his team gathered around a map of South Africa, pinned with red dots representing Johannesburg. Now, three new cities had green dots marking Cape Town, Durban, and Pretoria.

"These cities are gateways to influence," Vuruvayi said, running his finger over the map. "Cape Town is the seat of Parliament. Pretoria holds the national government. And Durban, with its ports, is a major hub for international trade. Together, they'll open doors we've never had access to."

The crew listened, absorbing his vision. The plan wasn't just about making money—it was about weaving a web of connections that could reshape the country from within.

Cape Town: The Seat of Power

Cape Town was their first target. It was a city with a vibrant community of activists and under-the-table deals, a place where government decisions were made that impacted all of South Africa. To infiltrate Cape Town, Vuruvayi focused on securing alliances with local influencers, especially those who distrusted the government and craved a more equitable society.

Linda's tech skills were crucial here. She infiltrated the city's digital infrastructure to uncover information on influential figures, corrupt officials, and those who might be sympathetic to their cause. They targeted a few key players in Cape Town's city council who had a history of shady deals. Instead of blackmail, they offered them a partnership: access to a portion of their growing wealth in exchange for political leverage.

To further integrate themselves into Cape Town's culture, they backed a local youth center, funded small businesses, and even supported a coastal cleanup project. These efforts gained them support among the city's residents, who saw them as outsiders but allies, there to help.

Durban: Control of the Ports

Durban, with its bustling port, was a gateway for goods entering and leaving the country. It was the perfect location for expanding their smuggling operations, using Durban's trade routes to quietly move items that could fund their projects. For this, Bheka took the lead. He had a history with port logistics and a keen sense of how to run complex supply chains without drawing attention.

Bheka approached a handful of warehouse owners who were struggling under the weight of rising taxes and overheads. He offered them a deal: a substantial monthly income in exchange for allowing a few unregistered goods to pass through unnoticed. The warehouse owners, wary but enticed, eventually agreed, and soon the crew had their own smuggling network within the port.

They also built ties with the dockworkers' union, which was feeling the sting of low wages and exploitative hours. Vuruvayi and his team provided resources to support the union's strikes, strengthening their relationship with workers who now saw them as advocates. This loyalty came in handy whenever the crew needed their shipments to slide by undetected.

Pretoria: Reaching the Heart of Government

Pretoria was the true nerve center, home to South Africa's national government. Getting a foothold here would be their most challenging and high-stakes move. They couldn't afford to be reckless; one wrong step could put them under national scrutiny.

For Pretoria, they took a subtler approach, focusing on information rather than money. Tumi leveraged her skills in psychology to connect with junior officials and aides in the government, charming her way into relationships that proved invaluable. She attended events, slipped into the social circles of politicians' families, and gathered secrets that could serve as leverage.

Meanwhile, Kabelo used his financial genius to quietly invest in a few well-placed consulting firms with government contracts. Through these channels, they could influence contracts and occasionally "lose" a paper trail. Whenever they needed government regulations bent, their allies in these firms could help ensure everything flowed smoothly.

Vuruvayi also knew that political influence would require subtlety and patience. They didn't attempt to sway every official but instead chose those whose loyalty could shift future decisions. It was a quiet infiltration, one that would take years to bear fruit but would secure their network against any potential threats from within the capital.

Strategic Cover Across the Map

As they built their influence in each city, the crew made sure their public image remained impeccable. Through their ongoing investments in youth programs, infrastructure, and healthcare in various townships, they gained a reputation as philanthropists, using their money to uplift communities. With each project, they strengthened ties with the residents, who, in return, were eager to shield them from outside eyes.

By strategically weaving together Cape Town's political edge, Durban's trade access, and Pretoria's government influence, the crew created a web that stretched across South Africa. Their operations were now secure not just in Johannesburg but throughout the country, with allies ready to intervene and support them whenever the need arose.

The National Network

Now, Vuruvayi's crew was no longer just a Johannesburg syndicate. They were a national network, a force that moved silently across South Africa, evading the law, gathering influence, and channeling money into causes that genuinely helped people.

Their reach was unprecedented, but they knew it would attract more attention. With each successful expansion, they were setting the stage for the next phase of their operation: to create a legacy of change and justice that could last even beyond their own lifetimes.

Chapter 19: International Allies

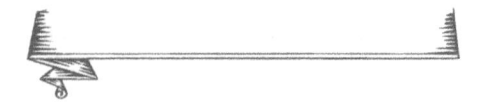

THE CREW'S INFLUENCE in South Africa was undeniable, their operations expanding from Johannesburg to Cape Town, Durban, and Pretoria. But as Vuruvayi looked beyond their accomplishments, he saw the potential for something even greater. With an international network, they could access resources and connections that would secure their hold on South Africa and protect them against any potential enemies.

Through his contacts in the Durban port, Vuruvayi learned of an international syndicate operating out of Europe and Southeast Asia. Known as "The Circle," the syndicate controlled smuggling routes, dealt in high-stakes information, and had its hand in covert operations across borders. The Circle rarely accepted new partnerships, but if Vuruvayi and his crew could prove themselves, the alliance could be mutually beneficial.

The First Connection

Vuruvayi's entry point was through an intermediary—a shipping magnate named Marco Moretti, a key associate of The Circle's operations in Africa. Marco operated discreetly, making alliances only with those who could demonstrate both skill and loyalty.

In a private meeting on Marco's yacht off the coast of Durban, Vuruvayi and his tech expert, Linda, presented their network's reach across South Africa. Linda showed Marco how they'd masked millions of rands' worth of transactions without a trace, an assurance that their crew could handle The Circle's covert demands without any leaks.

Marco listened, impressed. "You've built quite an empire for yourselves. But The Circle doesn't just need another group of thieves; we need partners who understand the risks and can protect themselves—and us."

Vuruvayi nodded. "We aren't just thieves. We're builders. Our goal is sustainable influence. If we partner with The Circle, your operations in Africa will be protected by the same reach that shields us. We'll exchange resources and keep each other strong."

After a moment of contemplation, Marco extended his hand. "We'll try this out, then. But remember, The Circle doesn't tolerate weakness or betrayal. One misstep, and the alliance ends—permanently."

A Test of Trust

To seal their partnership, The Circle required Vuruvayi's team to assist with a highly sensitive mission: securing a shipment of valuable, encrypted technology from Europe. It was due to arrive at the Durban port within days, but rival groups were also after it. The Circle wanted Vuruvayi's team to intercept and secure the shipment before it could be stolen by others.

For this mission, each member of Vuruvayi's crew had a crucial role. Linda hacked into the Durban port's surveillance to set up blind spots along the shipment's path. Bheka coordinated with local dockworkers to arrange for a secure location where they could hide the shipment temporarily. Tumi, with her skills in psychology, briefed a few key contacts on plausible stories in case anyone asked questions, while Kabelo handled the funds to ensure everyone involved was paid well and kept silent.

When the shipment arrived, the team executed flawlessly. The goods were transported to a hidden facility outside Durban before their rivals even realized it had docked. Vuruvayi informed Marco of the successful operation, and in return, The Circle promised them access to a secure offshore account that could handle the laundering of international funds without attracting unwanted scrutiny.

The Benefits of Alliance

With their alliance secured, Vuruvayi's crew began to benefit from The Circle's extensive resources. They gained access to specialized equipment, high-tech encryption tools for communications, and encrypted transport routes for moving money and goods. These resources strengthened their operations, allowing them to work seamlessly between cities and further shield themselves from detection.

In return, Vuruvayi's team provided The Circle with invaluable intel on South African corporations and politicians, particularly those who operated on the fringes of legality. Through Linda's cyber-infiltration skills, they accessed sensitive data and shared insights that The Circle could use to expand its influence within Africa.

New Horizons

The alliance with The Circle marked a turning point for Vuruvayi's crew. No longer were they bound by the limitations of operating solely within South Africa. Now, they had allies across borders, access to international funds, and the backing of one of the world's most formidable syndicates. They were not just South Africa's secret rulers; they were becoming part of a global network with eyes and ears in every major city.

For Vuruvayi, this alliance meant they could protect the communities they had invested in with a newfound strength. The Circle's resources allowed them to fortify their infrastructure and expand their community projects on a national scale, knowing they had a powerful safety net in place.

But Vuruvayi also knew that this partnership came with risks. The Circle's trust was conditional, and any missteps would be unforgivable. From this point on, every move would need to be carefully calculated. Their success was undeniable, but it would be their precision and loyalty to each other that would keep them alive in this ever-expanding empire of influence.

As the crew embraced their new international connections, they set their sights on transforming South Africa not just through crime, but through control, protection, and lasting influence. With The Circle as their allies, Vuruvayi and his team had become untouchable.

Chapter 20: High Society

WITH THEIR EMPIRE NOW reaching across South Africa and supported by international allies, Vuruvayi and his team understood that true power required more than underground influence; they needed to make a mark among the country's elite. Wealthy tycoons, influential politicians, and business moguls often attended private events that shaped the course of South Africa's future. If they could infiltrate these gatherings, they could gain valuable intelligence, identify potential adversaries, and even neutralize them before they became threats.

The plan was straightforward yet delicate: blend in, observe, and manipulate. But as outsiders, the crew needed to establish a new identity—a persona that would open doors into this elite circle.

Crafting Their Image

The crew carefully crafted personas that would fit seamlessly into high society. Vuruvayi assumed the role of a wealthy investor with mysterious international ties, a quiet but influential player who rarely spoke but observed everything. Tumi was cast as his refined companion, well-versed in politics and society. Bheka, with his knowledge of logistics, became an enigmatic businessman with holdings in shipping and transportation. Linda presented herself as a tech entrepreneur, a rising star known for disruptive ideas, while Kabelo played the role of a brilliant financier whose connections reached every major bank.

Their identities were meticulously created, complete with fabricated backgrounds, convincing business ventures, and a network of online profiles. With their new personas established, they began receiving invitations to high-society galas, private charity auctions, and exclusive cocktail parties where South Africa's wealthiest gathered.

The First Event: A Gala at the Carlton

The team's first venture was a high-profile charity gala held at the historic Carlton Hotel in Johannesburg. The event was organized by one of the country's most powerful businessmen, Leonard Du Plessis, who had deep ties to several industries. Du Plessis was known for both his wealth and ruthlessness, and he surrounded himself with allies who shared his vision of corporate dominance. He was the kind of man who could easily become a threat, and the crew was there to assess him closely.

Dressed in designer attire, the crew arrived in a sleek car, playing their roles to perfection. As they entered the ballroom, Vuruvayi took a moment to observe the room. Waiters circulated with trays of champagne, and the atmosphere buzzed with conversations of politics, business, and power plays. Linda immediately began scanning the room, mentally marking which guests were potential assets and which could become liabilities.

Outmaneuvering the Wealthy

As the night progressed, the crew split up, mingling with guests to gather information. Tumi effortlessly charmed a group of politicians, steering the conversation toward their financial backers and uncovering hidden alliances. Bheka, meanwhile, chatted with a logistics tycoon, subtly prying out details about security protocols used for high-value shipments—a tidbit that could come in handy for future operations.

Kabelo gravitated toward a group of bankers who were engrossed in discussions about offshore accounts and investment loopholes. He joined the conversation, skillfully dropping hints about lucrative international deals. Within minutes, he had earned their trust, securing connections that would later give the crew access to hidden banking channels.

Vuruvayi, true to his role, stayed quiet but kept a close eye on Du Plessis. He noticed how the businessman held court, surrounded by admirers and allies. Observing Du Plessis's behavior, Vuruvayi noted his arrogance and the way he dismissed certain people. He realized that while Du Plessis had power, his ego was a vulnerability that could be exploited.

A New Adversary

At one point in the evening, Vuruvayi overheard a conversation that caught his attention. Two guests were discussing a new, aggressive corporate figure who had been buying up properties across Johannesburg. This man, Anton Vermaak, was a rising star in real estate, known for hostile takeovers and his disregard for ethical practices. As the guests gossiped, Vuruvayi learned that Vermaak had plans to acquire properties in low-income areas, intending to displace residents for commercial development.

The information was concerning, as it posed a direct threat to some of the neighborhoods Vuruvayi's team had been supporting. He made a mental note to keep tabs on Vermaak and to intervene if his plans conflicted with their community projects. In his mind, Vermaak became an adversary—a symbol of greed and exploitation that Vuruvayi was determined to counter.

Turning Influencers into Allies

As the night wound down, Vuruvayi's team regrouped, having gathered intelligence that would open doors for future operations. But they knew that merely collecting information wasn't enough—they needed alliances. Over the next few weeks, they began fostering relationships with select members of high society, presenting themselves as potential business partners who shared similar interests.

Linda arranged private tech demonstrations for prominent investors, impressing them with her expertise and sparking their interest in her "company." Tumi hosted intimate dinners with the politicians she had met, listening to their ambitions and subtly guiding them towards goals that aligned with the crew's plans. Kabelo provided strategic financial insights to his new banking contacts, positioning himself as someone they could trust with their wealth.

Soon, the crew had built a network within high society. They had turned influential figures into allies, people who would provide them with insider information, cover up their tracks, and even shield them from investigations should suspicions arise.

High Society as a Shield

Through their presence in high society, Vuruvayi's team gained access to information that kept them one step ahead of potential threats. They discovered plans for new police initiatives targeting organized crime, upcoming political maneuvers, and shifting corporate alliances. Whenever a competitor or adversary considered challenging them, the crew used their network to strategically outmaneuver them, ensuring their operations remained secure.

The crew had become invisible in plain sight, protected by the very people who once saw themselves as untouchable. They were no longer just criminals; they were insiders in the world of wealth and power, operating under a shield woven from trust, influence, and deception.

In this new sphere, Vuruvayi's team could move freely, gathering intelligence, neutralizing threats, and expanding their empire with ease. They had truly become untouchable, masters not only of the criminal underworld but of South Africa's elite circles.

Part 3: Building Legacy and Avoiding Capture

Chapter 21: Ultimate Betrayal

AS THEIR EMPIRE GREW and influence expanded, the inner circle of Vuruvayi's team appeared as tight-knit and unbreakable as ever. But with wealth, power, and the ever-present danger of exposure, cracks began to form, small at first, but just enough to breed mistrust. For one of Vuruvayi's trusted friends, the weight of their criminal life started to feel like a burden that could collapse at any moment, taking them all down.

Kabelo, the financial genius, had always been driven by ambition and self-preservation. As the crew's influence spread and their schemes became increasingly complex, he started questioning if their loyalty to Vuruvayi was worth the risks. He watched as Vuruvayi's influence extended beyond South Africa, and though Kabelo was proud of their achievements, a part of him grew wary. Their leader's vision had always been inspiring, but it also felt insatiable, and that relentless hunger started to unnerve Kabelo. The question echoed in his mind: could this empire they'd built crumble in a single moment if Vuruvayi misstepped?

The Temptation of an Out

One night, after a successful venture that brought them millions, Kabelo was approached by a shadowy figure from an old rival syndicate. The man hinted at a lucrative offer—a way out with a substantial cut and immunity from prosecution. All it would require was a bit of information—something minor at first, like a list of Vuruvayi's upcoming movements or the locations of their secure accounts. The syndicate promised Kabelo his freedom in exchange, along with protection should he decide to turn against his team.

Kabelo's thoughts raced. Freedom had always seemed out of reach, and here it was, tempting him, waiting for him to reach out. Could he finally walk away and secure his safety, even if it meant betraying the man who had built their empire?

Over the next few days, Kabelo wrestled with his thoughts. The life they led was thrilling, but it came with constant threats of exposure, capture, or worse. He could never fully relax, always looking over his shoulder, wondering when their fortune would run out. He began pulling back, less engaged with the team and more withdrawn during meetings. The others noticed, but no one mentioned it—no one, except Vuruvayi.

Confrontation and Redemption

Vuruvayi had always been perceptive, especially when it came to his friends. Kabelo's sudden change in behavior didn't escape his notice, and it didn't take long for him to connect the dots. Vuruvayi confronted Kabelo during a quiet moment at their hideout. In a calm but serious tone, he asked, "Kabelo, what's going on with you? We've come too far to start having secrets now."

Kabelo hesitated, but seeing Vuruvayi's unwavering gaze, he felt the weight of his thoughts spill over. He admitted his doubts, his concerns about the endless risks, and the offer he'd received. He confessed the temptation of a quieter, safer life away from the constant threat of capture.

Vuruvayi listened, his expression unreadable. When Kabelo finished, Vuruvayi's voice was steady. "I get it, Kabelo. We're in a dangerous game. I'd be lying if I said I haven't thought about what this life could cost us all. But this empire—it's as much yours as it is mine. I can't build it without you. None of us can."

He went on, sharing his vision not as a leader commanding loyalty, but as a friend asking for trust. Vuruvayi reminded Kabelo of why they started: to prove that they could rise above their circumstances, to take power into their own hands, and to use it not only for themselves but for the people they had vowed to uplift. He told Kabelo that if he wanted out, he wouldn't stop him—but that he would always be welcomed back, no matter where he went.

Moved by Vuruvayi's words, Kabelo felt the tension lift. He realized that his loyalty wasn't just to the empire or the money but to the shared purpose they had built together. In that moment, he saw Vuruvayi not as a ruthless mastermind but as a friend who would sacrifice for his people.

Strengthening the Bond

With the air cleared, Vuruvayi called a meeting, where he and Kabelo laid everything bare. They told the crew about the rival syndicate's attempt to turn Kabelo and how close they'd come to breaking apart. The honesty forged a new level of trust within the group. Everyone felt the weight of what they had to lose but also the strength of the bond that had kept them together through every heist, every risk, every close call.

The team developed new protocols to guard against internal and external threats. They reinforced their code, reminding themselves that loyalty to each other was their greatest asset. They understood now that the only way to secure their legacy was through unity, as strong as steel and just as unbreakable.

For Kabelo, it was a moment of clarity. He recommitted to Vuruvayi and the rest of the crew, vowing that he would never again let doubt cloud his loyalty. The betrayal that had almost torn them apart had instead forged them into something even stronger.

From that day on, they moved forward with renewed resolve, prepared to outwit anyone who dared stand in their way. They would protect each other, protect their empire, and see their shared dream through to the end—no matter what.

Chapter 22: The Clandestine Operation

THE SPRAWLING PORT city of Durban had become a hub of opportunities and challenges for Vuruvayi and his team. Known for its vibrant economy and strategic coastal access, it was a prize many sought to control. But this time, the stakes were higher than ever. The authorities, catching whispers of a major heist in planning stages, had flooded the city with police and set up strict checkpoints. The city was on high alert, and every move Vuruvayi's team made would be scrutinized.

Yet, that didn't stop them. They knew that if they could pull off an operation here, under the most watchful eyes, their legend would grow to new heights. And for Vuruvayi, it wasn't just about the money or even the thrill—it was about cementing their legacy as the crew that no one could capture or stop.

The Target: Durban's Exclusive Diamond Vault

Durban's bustling coastline was home to more than just industry; a wealthy local magnate had established a private vault for high-profile clients who wanted to store precious jewels, primarily diamonds. It was heavily guarded and rumored to be impenetrable, protected by layers of security designed by South Africa's finest tech experts. But the vault wasn't the only target; they planned to hit the vault and, in parallel, raid a shipment of cash bound for one of Durban's biggest banks.

Each step had to be flawless, synchronized down to the second. With the city teeming with police and the stakes sky-high, any miscalculation could bring their empire crashing down.

The Plan

With weeks of preparation, Vuruvayi's crew crafted a plan more daring and intricate than anything they'd done before. Each member's skills would be tested to their limits, and failure was not an option. Their tech genius, Linda, was tasked with hacking into Durban's public security network, rerouting cameras and distorting feeds at critical points. Tumi, the psychological mastermind, would distract authorities by planting false leads, sending anonymous tips about "other" operations taking place in opposite parts of the city. Meanwhile, Bheka would coordinate the logistics, ensuring their exit routes and contingencies were airtight.

But this time, Kabelo's role was even more delicate. His job wasn't just to handle finances but to manage the transfer of funds through offshore channels in real-time, minimizing any traceable transactions.

A City on Alert

The night of the heist arrived. Under the cover of darkness, they moved into position. Linda had already triggered minor security alerts across the city to divert police forces. In response, patrols and checkpoints sprang up across Durban, spreading the authorities thin. They couldn't afford to ignore any threat, which gave Vuruvayi and his team just the window they needed.

As Vuruvayi and Tumi made their way to the vault, Linda took control of the city's surveillance feeds, creating a digital smokescreen that masked their movements. At the same time, Bheka kept a close watch on police radio channels, ready to alert them of any shift in patrols or unexpected movements.

Infiltrating the Vault

Reaching the vault required navigating a labyrinth of locked doors, armed guards, and state-of-the-art security systems. Linda guided them through with precision, feeding them real-time details as they bypassed laser grids and high-tech sensors. The vault's final layer, a biometric lock, required fingerprints and a retinal scan, both of which Linda had obtained through an elaborate scheme involving a digital forgery and data extracted from an insider.

The vault opened, revealing rows of safety deposit boxes filled with jewels. Working swiftly, Vuruvayi and Tumi loaded the diamonds into secured cases. Linda disabled the alarm system temporarily, giving them exactly seven minutes before it would auto-reset.

The Diversion: Raiding the Shipment

Meanwhile, across the city, Bheka and Kabelo executed the second part of the operation. The shipment of cash was being transported in an armored convoy guarded by heavily armed personnel. With the police spread thin, they timed the interception perfectly, attacking at a precise blind spot in the route Linda had mapped.

Bheka and Kabelo's precision was remarkable. They disabled the convoy with minimal force, transferring the cash into a disguised truck that blended into regular traffic. The entire heist took less than four minutes, leaving no clues or witnesses.

The Escape

With both the diamonds and cash secured, Vuruvayi signaled the crew to initiate the escape. Linda restored the surveillance feeds, ensuring no one could trace their moves. As they rendezvoused at a remote location, the city's alarms sounded, police scrambling to contain what they thought was a localized incident.

But Vuruvayi's team was already gone, their exit meticulously planned. They split up into smaller vehicles, each taking a different route out of Durban, evading checkpoints and blending into the early morning traffic. The city was still buzzing with alerts when the crew quietly regrouped miles outside of Durban, safe and undetected.

The Aftermath

News of the heist rocked South Africa. Authorities were left scrambling, piecing together fragments of security footage and scrambled feeds, all of which led nowhere. The police's heightened alert had only made the crew's success more remarkable; they had pulled off the impossible in a city that was watching every move.

For Vuruvayi and his team, the Durban heist was more than just another score. It was proof that they were untouchable, capable of taking on any city, any system, and winning. As they split the spoils, their loyalty deepened, bound by the shared knowledge that together, they were unstoppable. Their empire grew stronger, their influence spread further, and their legend as South Africa's untouchable crew was cemented once more.

The Clandestine Operation would be whispered about for years to come, a feat of flawless execution under the most intense conditions. And for Vuruvayi, it was yet another step toward an empire that would outlast them all.

Chapter 23: Johannesburg's Benefactors

AFTER THE SUCCESS OF their daring heists, Vuruvayi and his team amassed enough wealth to rival major corporations. But instead of basking in luxury and flaunting their riches, they turned their focus toward their roots. Vuruvayi had never forgotten where he came from, nor the struggles of the people he grew up with. He knew that true power lay not only in wealth but in the impact he could have on those around him. With the crew's blessings, he decided to reinvest heavily into Daveyton and surrounding townships, transforming themselves into benefactors for the communities that needed it most.

The Plan to Give Back

From the start, the team had committed to a code—one that allowed them to steal from the corrupt and reinvest in the underserved. Now that they had the means, they put together an ambitious plan to uplift the townships around Johannesburg. Vuruvayi gathered the crew, laying out a detailed vision that spanned everything from education and healthcare to small business development.

"We're going to give people the chances we never had," he said, the conviction in his voice resonating with each of them. "And we'll do it in a way that makes them proud, that reminds them of their own strength."

Rebuilding the Heart of Daveyton

Their first step was revitalizing Daveyton, where Vuruvayi and most of his crew had their roots. They launched initiatives to repair infrastructure, refurbishing schools, clinics, and community centers.

They brought in skilled workers from the area, offering fair wages and empowering locals to become part of the change. The work progressed quickly, the team pouring resources into each project to ensure top-quality improvements.

To honor the community's spirit, they focused on projects that celebrated local culture. Public murals and sculptures went up in the main squares, depicting the history and resilience of the people. Community leaders, initially skeptical of the sudden investment, began to see the tangible results and threw their support behind the mysterious benefactors.

Educational Empowerment

Vuruvayi had always valued knowledge, and he knew that education could change lives. Partnering with local educators, he and Kabelo spearheaded initiatives to provide scholarships and free vocational training. New computer labs sprang up in schools, each stocked with equipment they'd purchased through carefully hidden offshore accounts. They provided resources for teachers and learning materials for students, aiming to give young people a chance to break the cycles of poverty and build a future.

Recognizing the challenges faced by the youth, they didn't just stop at academics. They funded after-school programs that offered mentorship, sports, and art, giving young people a constructive outlet and keeping them away from the dangers of gang influence.

Healthcare and Welfare Initiatives

With Linda's strategic thinking and Tumi's people skills, the crew moved into healthcare next. They funded clinics, bringing in doctors and health professionals willing to provide low-cost or free services to the community. Mobile health units began operating in areas that previously had little access to healthcare, ensuring that even the most isolated families received attention.

Mental health was another area often overlooked in impoverished communities, so Tumi organized counseling services and support groups. The crew even funded outreach programs for people struggling with addiction, making resources available to anyone seeking a path toward a better life.

Economic Growth and Small Business Support

Recognizing that sustainable change meant empowering the local economy, Vuruvayi's crew set up a fund to support small businesses. They provided low-interest loans to local entrepreneurs with strong ideas but little access to capital. The crew helped aspiring business owners open everything from corner stores to tech startups, sparking a wave of economic growth across Daveyton and beyond.

Bheka, with his logistical expertise, managed the supply chains, ensuring every business had the tools and connections needed to succeed. His experience in operations helped countless small businesses expand and reach markets they'd previously struggled to enter.

Vuruvayi and his team took it a step further, setting up a local cooperative that allowed these small businesses to pool resources, cutting costs and increasing their reach. From butchers to seamstresses, the community began to thrive, buoyed by the financial lifeline their mysterious benefactors had offered.

Becoming Local Heroes

As the projects expanded and the results became evident, word spread like wildfire. People spoke about the shadowy heroes who had come to Daveyton's aid, uplifted their communities, and provided opportunities that had long been out of reach. The media caught wind of it too, running stories that marveled at the transformation taking place in these previously neglected townships.

Despite the secrecy surrounding their identities, people began calling them Johannesburg's "modern-day Robin Hoods." Vuruvayi's crew had managed to stay anonymous, but the gratitude and respect of the people were palpable. They had become legends—beloved benefactors whose generosity was helping rebuild communities and restore hope.

Shifting Public Perception

For Vuruvayi, the success of these projects was proof that their heists had been worth the risk. By reinvesting in the community, they had made an undeniable impact, something far more lasting than just money. And with each improvement, their immunity grew stronger; no one in the townships would betray them, and even the police found it harder to pursue a crew viewed as local heroes.

Their influence expanded beyond Daveyton to neighboring townships, where communities began requesting similar investments. Each step of the way, they took on projects that aligned with their code—always building up, never exploiting.

In a city that had once looked upon them as outlaws, Vuruvayi and his team had earned a reputation as protectors, defenders of those who'd been forgotten by society. They continued their operations under the radar, keeping Johannesburg on edge while uplifting those who needed it most.

They knew that as long as they had the people's loyalty, they would remain untouchable, their empire secured not just by wealth, but by the faith of those they had uplifted.

Chapter 24: Heist Unraveled

DESPITE ALL OF VURUVAYI'S crew's careful planning, near-flawless execution, and impeccable cover stories, the law had finally found a crack. Over the past few months, the police had intensified their investigations, desperate to track down Johannesburg's elusive benefactors-turned-criminal masterminds. With the media fascination growing and whispers of a modern-day Robin Hood crew sweeping across South Africa, pressure on law enforcement was at an all-time high.

One night, as Vuruvayi was reviewing their recent investments in a makeshift office, he received an unexpected message from Linda: "They're onto us."

It turned out that a minor slip during their heist in Durban had gone unnoticed by the crew but not by a persistent investigator. A single piece of digital evidence, a fragment of Linda's security interference on a bank's internal systems, had resurfaced. The detail was minuscule, but it was enough for the police to trace back some of the electronic interference patterns, connecting dots between heists across multiple cities.

The Breakthrough

Captain Themba Maseko, a sharp, determined detective known for his tenacity, had been leading the case from day one. He'd lost countless hours combing through reports, camera feeds, and financial transactions. While Vuruvayi's team had left almost no clues behind, Themba noticed one peculiar pattern in the bank's firewall breach logs from Durban. It mirrored another breach in Johannesburg that the crew had executed months prior.

Using this lead, Themba and his team pieced together a trail of digital breadcrumbs. Linda's tech had always been top-tier, but the software she'd used had, unknowingly, left an identifiable signature. Themba matched this digital pattern across multiple heists, and it led him to suspect that each of these robberies was the work of the same group.

Internal Panic

When Linda shared the news with the crew, a tense silence settled among them. They had built their empire on the premise that they were untouchable. They had invested heavily in communities to keep people loyal and even bought their way out of potential betrayals. But this was different. This wasn't a rumor or speculation; this was hard evidence that could expose their entire operation.

Vuruvayi felt the weight of the realization settle heavily on him. For the first time in years, his confidence wavered. He gathered the team in a safe house just outside Johannesburg, far from prying eyes, where they could strategize in peace.

"We've been careful, maybe even too careful. But this means nothing if they can trace us," Vuruvayi said, looking each member in the eye. "What matters now is how we respond."

A Plan for Survival

Linda immediately set to work, reviewing every piece of technology she'd used in past heists to identify what had gone wrong. Meanwhile, Tumi, the psychology mastermind, worked on contingency plans to protect their network of allies and corrupt officials, ensuring no one would turn on them if questioned.

Bheka and Kabelo went over their finances and businesses with fine-tooth precision, redirecting resources and cutting ties to minimize any direct connection to the crew. They liquidated assets, dissolved fake identities, and rerouted offshore accounts to remove any visible trace of their activities.

"We need to go dark," Vuruvayi said, his voice steady with resolve. "No more heists until we're absolutely sure we're safe. We focus on cleanup. We don't give Themba or anyone else a single scrap to work with."

The Pressure Builds

Meanwhile, Captain Themba Maseko was building a case, one that included the crew's pattern of activity across multiple cities. His research painted a picture of how the group funded community projects and bought loyalty in Johannesburg and beyond. To him, they were skilled, dangerous manipulators hiding behind a veneer of philanthropy. With this newfound evidence, he was more determined than ever to expose them.

But even with his breakthrough, Themba found himself struggling against mounting obstacles. The communities viewed the mysterious benefactors as heroes and became tight-lipped whenever he or his team tried to gather information. And each time he got close to someone on the crew's payroll, they vanished or recanted statements. He sensed the pull of Vuruvayi's influence, but it only made him more committed.

The Crew Strikes Back

Rather than wait for Themba to close in, Vuruvayi decided they needed to take a more aggressive approach. They planned a counterattack, something subtle but effective enough to destabilize the investigation without drawing suspicion.

Linda launched a campaign of digital disinformation, feeding the police false leads and planting fake connections to other crime syndicates. Tumi, meanwhile, anonymously reached out to influential journalists, subtly suggesting that the police were wasting resources and stirring up rumors that the authorities were targeting community heroes for the sake of corporate interests. The press, already intrigued by the Robin Hood-like activities, eagerly ran with the narrative.

The Tension Mounts

As Themba's investigation stalled under mounting public scrutiny, Vuruvayi and his team knew they had managed to buy themselves some time. But the pressure was undeniable. They had come too close to exposure, and the experience left them shaken, realizing that even their meticulously crafted plans had vulnerabilities.

Sitting with his team, Vuruvayi made a final decision. They would tighten security even further, sparingly choose future targets, and focus on reinforcing their networks. The crew was committed to their code, their cause, and their impact on communities. But now, they understood the risk they would always carry.

From that day forward, Vuruvayi operated with a new resolve. He knew that as long as they walked the line between hero and outlaw, they would need to be prepared for close calls like this one. And with his team beside him, he was ready for whatever came next, for they would either go down as heroes in the people's eyes or as legends who could never be caught.

Chapter 25: Covering Tracks

THE CLOSE CALL WITH Captain Themba Maseko's investigation had left Vuruvayi and his crew reeling. They knew they had to act fast to throw the police off their scent completely. It was time to turn the game of cat and mouse in their favor by creating an elaborate web of false evidence—one that would not only mislead the authorities but also make them chase shadows in circles.

Vuruvayi and his team pooled their resources and devised a plan to plant evidence that would connect their heists to rival criminal networks. By doing this, they hoped to redirect the attention away from Johannesburg's Robin Hoods and onto groups that were already on law enforcement's radar.

Manufacturing a Paper Trail

Kabelo, the finance genius, took the lead. Using their offshore accounts, he meticulously crafted a series of financial transactions that linked a significant amount of their "earnings" to various shell companies associated with suspected crime syndicates. He studied the financial patterns of these organizations and imitated their methods—hiding deposits through layers of fake companies and anonymous accounts.

Under Kabelo's watch, funds were redirected through obscure transactions, and false trails were left, suggesting money transfers to high-profile criminal figures outside South Africa. He even created phony loan agreements, tying the shell companies to illegal enterprises abroad. These documents were carefully planted in digital records that he knew the authorities could eventually access, creating the illusion that their money flowed through criminal empires.

Creating Physical Evidence

Meanwhile, Bheka, with his logistical mind, worked on planting physical evidence. They rented safehouses under assumed names, each designed to look like a base of operations for the alleged syndicates. He filled these locations with fake "plans" for robberies, counterfeit money, surveillance photos of banks, and maps with markings on potential targets. These materials were carefully constructed to resemble the methods of each rival gang, down to the tiniest details.

At one location, Bheka left behind staged fingerprints and hair samples, using items they'd bought second-hand to throw investigators further off course. He even went so far as to hire actors to pose as suspicious individuals, leaving them in places where undercover cops could notice them, ensuring that the trail pointed to well-known gang leaders.

Digital Diversion

Linda, their tech expert, was in her element. She created digital footprints, placing fake emails, encrypted messages, and online "chats" between key players in Johannesburg's underground. The messages hinted at elaborate plans to destabilize certain banks and conduct high-level heists across South Africa. She also hacked into minor gang databases, subtly planting information that would align with the police's discoveries.

To make the deception foolproof, Linda used IP addresses from various countries to create fake "logins" and access points for these fabricated digital records. Each login was timed to match the dates of their previous heists, effectively framing rival gangs without any connection to the Robin Hood crew. If investigators tried to trace her steps, they would only end up with leads that pointed overseas or toward gangs with no known affiliations to Vuruvayi's crew.

Setting the Trap

Once the team felt their false evidence was in place, Tumi used his connections to spread rumors in the criminal underworld. Carefully, he planted whispers that there were high-ranking criminals planning attacks on banks across Johannesburg. Tumi knew that word would eventually make its way back to the police, adding credibility to the false evidence they had created.

The police, already on high alert, were quick to act. Captain Themba Maseko, sensing a major breakthrough, shifted his focus to the supposed criminal networks that seemed to match his team's findings. With mounting "proof" and witness rumors connecting them to the heists, the investigation shifted dramatically away from Vuruvayi's crew.

The Power of Perception

News of the ongoing police crackdown on these "rival" gangs reached the public, sparking an outcry. The media painted a dramatic picture of these criminal syndicates, describing them as ruthless and calling for swift action from law enforcement. Meanwhile, whispers about the benevolent benefactors of Johannesburg continued, with people still singing their praises.

For Vuruvayi and his team, watching the media frenzy from the sidelines was both a relief and a reminder of their own vulnerability. They had successfully turned the tide in their favor, creating a firewall of deception that protected their true identities. The police would now spend months chasing false leads and scrutinizing gang networks that had nothing to do with the Robin Hoods of Johannesburg.

A Renewed Sense of Caution

After covering their tracks, Vuruvayi gathered his team for a final briefing, reinforcing the need for caution in all their future moves.

"We got lucky this time, but we won't always be able to rely on luck," he said, his gaze steely. "From here on, everything we do is airtight. We stay out of sight, work from the shadows, and make sure nothing links back to us."

The close call had taught them a valuable lesson: no matter how skilled they were, no empire was truly untouchable. With their tracks carefully covered and their operation shielded behind layers of false evidence, Vuruvayi and his team were ready to continue their work, more cautious and more determined than ever.

Chapter 26: Uplifting SA's Future

WITH THEIR EMPIRE PROTECTED and their tracks carefully covered, Vuruvayi and his crew shifted focus toward a mission close to their hearts: uplifting the communities of South Africa. They'd amassed a fortune, but to Vuruvayi, wealth meant nothing unless it could fuel a brighter future for others who, like him, had grown up with limited opportunities.

In a quiet meeting in their Daveyton safehouse, Vuruvayi laid out his vision for transforming the lives of young South Africans. "It's time we invest in the people. A community that grows together is a community that's strong enough to change its future."

The Scholarship Program

The crew began by establishing scholarships for students across South Africa. Kabelo, the finance genius, set up a foundation under a legitimate cover to ensure anonymity. He sourced funds from their various shell companies, funneling the money into scholarships for underprivileged students with academic potential but limited means.

Vuruvayi knew that many young people in the townships had dreams beyond the narrow options available to them. Through the scholarship program, they offered fully funded opportunities in fields like engineering, medicine, information technology, and the arts. For many recipients, the scholarship was a life-changing chance to leave hardship behind and pursue careers that could uplift their families and communities.

Youth Centers and Skill Development

While scholarships helped those excelling in academics, Vuruvayi wanted to reach the broader youth population. With Tumi's help, they identified neighborhoods most in need of youth engagement programs. Vuruvayi's crew invested in building youth centers in major townships, each one equipped with resources for skill development.

These centers became safe havens where young people could learn computer skills, coding, carpentry, and entrepreneurship. They held workshops on financial literacy and job preparation, guiding young people away from paths of crime and desperation. Each center was staffed by teachers and mentors who had risen from similar circumstances, creating a strong support system for every attendee.

As the centers grew in popularity, they became hubs of hope in their communities, attracting hundreds of young South Africans eager to improve their futures. For Vuruvayi and his team, seeing the centers thrive was a personal victory—a visible proof that their influence could be used for more than just amassing wealth.

Libraries for Knowledge and Growth

Bheka, who had a love for reading, championed the idea of building libraries across townships. He knew that access to books had opened his own mind, and he was determined to offer that same access to others. They scouted locations in under-resourced areas and funded the construction of small libraries, each filled with a curated selection of books on history, business, science, and literature.

In addition to traditional books, the libraries included digital learning stations with internet access, enabling people to expand their knowledge far beyond their surroundings. For many communities, these libraries became the first stepping stone toward academic growth and self-education.

Long-Lasting Change

Word of the scholarships, youth centers, and libraries spread like wildfire, creating a ripple effect across South Africa. People were inspired by the mysterious benefactors who had quietly uplifted communities without seeking recognition or credit. Local media outlets, unaware of Vuruvayi's criminal enterprise, lauded these "angel investors" as champions of the people.

Meanwhile, Vuruvayi and his team watched their vision take root from the shadows, deeply satisfied with the legacy they were building. They saw themselves as silent architects of a brighter South Africa, using their wealth to fight the inequalities that had once held them back.

Strengthening Community Bonds

By investing in youth and education, Vuruvayi's crew strengthened their bond with local communities, who now saw them not only as benefactors but as protectors. Their generosity cultivated loyalty and gratitude, further securing the crew's position as untouchable figures in the eyes of those they served.

As they walked through townships and saw children learning, young people finding their passions, and elders smiling in appreciation, Vuruvayi knew that their investments were laying the foundation for future generations. His empire might have been built in the shadows, but its legacy would shine brightly across South Africa for years to come.

Chapter 27: Blurring the Line

THE IMPACT OF VURUVAYI and his crew's philanthropy swept across South Africa like a wave, reaching far beyond the townships they had invested in. From Cape Town to Johannesburg, Durban to Pretoria, communities whispered about the mysterious benefactors who built youth centers, funded scholarships, and brought libraries to underfunded schools. The contrast between their criminal underworld and their community investments stirred a nationwide debate—were these masked philanthropists criminals or heroes?

The Public Divide

As stories of their charity surfaced, so did rumors about the origins of the funds. Talk show hosts and journalists debated endlessly, some praising the group as modern-day Robin Hoods, while others condemned their illicit activities. Media outlets picked up on the duality of their actions, with headlines that posed questions rather than answers: *"Crime Syndicate or Saviors?"* and *"Heroes of Johannesburg or Shadows of Corruption?"*

In community halls and street corners, South Africans engaged in heated discussions. For many in the townships, Vuruvayi's crew were saviors—people who used their money and influence to uplift those who had been left behind by the system. They had built up areas the government had long ignored, bringing education, opportunity, and a renewed sense of hope.

Others, however, were less sympathetic. They argued that money born of crime would inevitably taint those it touched, regardless of how it was used. Community elders, clergy members, and those who had been affected by violence in the city were wary of glorifying criminals. The debate revealed a profound moral dilemma: Could good deeds erase the harm caused by their criminal origins?

Media Propaganda and Misdirection

Linda, the team's tech genius, kept a close eye on media trends and social sentiment. She knew the dangers of public scrutiny and orchestrated a counter-narrative online. Using fake accounts and bots, she spread stories that emphasized the positive impact of their investments, sharing testimonials from scholarship recipients, youth center graduates, and community leaders who had benefited from the mysterious benefactors.

Through these stories, they painted a picture of a caring, Robin Hood-like group who took from the corrupt and gave back to those in need. While Linda's efforts didn't erase the whispers of criminality, they shifted the spotlight onto their good deeds, softening the public's view and causing many to question whether their methods truly mattered if the outcomes were positive.

Personal Reflection and Doubt

Within the crew, the debate struck a chord as well. As they saw South Africa split over their actions, some of Vuruvayi's friends felt conflicted. Kabelo, the finance genius, couldn't ignore the irony that the money he had helped steal was now paying for the very opportunities he and his community had once been denied. Bheka, who had grown up idolizing great leaders and activists, wondered if their actions really aligned with the vision of a better South Africa.

One night, as the team gathered, Vuruvayi sensed the doubts among his friends. He addressed them with a somber resolve. "Yes, we've broken laws. But those laws were never written for people like us. They were written to protect the wealthy, to keep the power in their hands. We've done what we had to do to make real change. If the price is being called criminals, then so be it."

His words struck a chord, reassuring some while leaving others still uncertain. The debate over their legacy, however, reminded them of the fine line they walked between villainy and heroism—a line they blurred with every act of charity and every heist.

Gaining Unintentional Allies

As the public conversation continued, they found unexpected allies in certain government officials who, fed up with bureaucracy and corruption, saw the value in the work Vuruvayi's team was doing. While they couldn't openly support criminals, these officials subtly shifted focus away from their activities, allowing the crew to operate with less interference.

This unofficial protection gave Vuruvayi and his friends more freedom, but it also complicated the public perception even further. Was the government condoning crime by allowing these masked benefactors to continue? Were they failing to enforce justice, or was there an unspoken understanding that some changes simply required unconventional means?

A Legacy in Question

As their influence grew, so did the divide in public opinion. Vuruvayi's crew became a symbol of rebellion, an embodiment of South Africa's complex relationship with justice, survival, and empowerment. In one breath, they were called criminals, in another, heroes. And as the nation watched them leave their mark, it became clear that their legacy would not be a simple one.

For Vuruvayi, the blurring line between good and bad, hero and villain, didn't deter him. If anything, it validated his belief that change often came at a cost—and sometimes that cost was the world's understanding of who you really were. In the end, the lives they had transformed stood as evidence of their purpose, and whether viewed as saviors or shadows, Vuruvayi knew their legacy would be felt long after they had disappeared from the public eye.

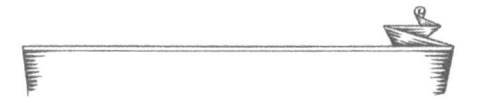

Chapter 28: A City in Their Pockets

WITH YEARS OF CAREFULLY crafted influence, strategic bribes, and well-placed connections, Vuruvayi's crew had turned Johannesburg into a machine that worked in their favor. It was a city in their pockets, its gears greased by the wealth and sway of their criminal empire. Police officers, city officials, even local politicians—each one bound by favors, loyalty, or fear—had a part to play in ensuring that Vuruvayi's team operated smoothly and discreetly.

The Network of Influence

In the heart of Johannesburg, a web of allies protected them. Linda had masterfully built up a network of officials who looked the other way, lawyers who could untangle any legal snare, and law enforcement officers who would tip them off before any raid. But it wasn't just about bribes; it was about loyalty and mutual benefit. Many officials saw Vuruvayi's group as more than criminals—they were benefactors who delivered real improvements that the government often neglected. Hospitals saw new equipment, community centers received funding, and schools found surprise grants—all anonymously underwritten by the wealth of Vuruvayi's empire.

With these acts, Vuruvayi had positioned his group as indispensable allies to Johannesburg's civil servants, who privately believed that some order, even a shadowy one, was better than the chaos that had existed before. The city's elite operated with their blessing, as long as the favors continued to flow.

Bribing the Gatekeepers

Kabelo, with his sharp mind for finance, managed their "influence budget" with meticulous care. He ensured that every bribe was paid under layers of shell companies and offshore accounts. Junior officers received small perks—a paid holiday, a bonus for their children's school fees—while higher-ranking officials got regular "gifts" that secured their continued loyalty. For certain city council members, Kabelo even arranged business opportunities, backchannel investments, or placements in lucrative private companies. These deals effectively transformed them into stakeholders in Vuruvayi's underworld empire.

Thanks to Kabelo's strategic investments, Johannesburg's inner workings became increasingly tied to the crew's success. People in power now had a vested interest in keeping Vuruvayi's team in operation. It was no longer about bribes alone; they were partners, their fates subtly linked to the empire they'd once sworn to destroy.

Strategic Misdirection

While Linda managed the technology and surveillance, Tumi, the psychology genius, ensured that every move was calculated to keep them hidden in plain sight. She understood how to manipulate perception, ensuring that the crew's operations were always one step removed from public suspicion. Tumi established "decoy" projects—small, seemingly suspicious events—that drew attention away from their real objectives.

When whispers of corruption surfaced in local newspapers, she orchestrated scandals involving smaller, unrelated groups, letting the media run wild with fabricated stories. By controlling the narrative, Tumi ensured that any attention on their crew was brief and ultimately redirected. In the public's eye, Johannesburg's troubles seemed like the work of countless small-time players, not a masterfully orchestrated shadow empire.

Unspoken Rules and Mutual Dependence

In time, the crew's influence reached such heights that their relationship with the city's officials became an unspoken agreement.

They had created a delicate balance—a city of whispered alliances, where everyone knew their role. Officials who had once turned a blind eye now depended on the crew's continued operations. Hospitals and schools counted on their anonymous donations; even certain municipal projects ran on funds Vuruvayi had quietly funneled through his network.

But the loyalty they commanded wasn't solely out of self-interest. Many officials, especially those who had grown up in Johannesburg's struggling communities, saw Vuruvayi's crew as part of a new era. Unlike the faceless corporations and distant politicians who had failed them, Vuruvayi's team was tangible, present, and surprisingly invested in the city's wellbeing. They fixed potholes, improved safety in neglected neighborhoods, and brought light to places once forgotten by the system.

A Shadow Government

In effect, Vuruvayi's team had created a shadow government within Johannesburg. They had the power to get things done faster than any bureaucratic process. If someone needed a permit, a call to Vuruvayi's contacts could ensure it was expedited. If a business wanted protection, they knew who to approach. And if the police needed help solving a violent case, an anonymous tip from Vuruvayi's network would arrive just in time.

Johannesburg became their fortress, the people's loyalty mixed with admiration and fear. While the city thrived under their hidden hand, they knew their control was precarious. A single betrayal, a misstep, or an ambitious outsider could bring their empire crashing down. Yet, for now, Vuruvayi and his friends stood as the silent rulers of Johannesburg, wielding power beyond any official's reach.

In that moment, they understood the paradox they had created. Though criminals by definition, they had become the city's protectors, preserving a fragile order that no one dared to question. And while they knew it couldn't last forever, for now, Johannesburg worked for them—and as long as it did, they intended to use every ounce of power they had to keep it that way.

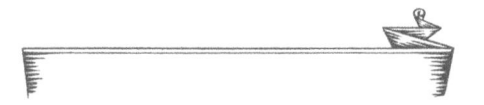

Chapter 29: The Final Operation

AS THE YEARS PASSED, Vuruvayi and his crew had achieved more than they'd ever imagined. They held Johannesburg in their pockets, with influence extending beyond the city to other South African metropolises. Yet, the weight of their actions, the countless nights spent evading capture, and the constant need for secrecy had begun to wear on them. It was time to end the game. They all agreed: they would pull off one last operation, a score so massive it would set them up for life and allow them to disappear with enough wealth to live freely—and, as always, to reinvest in the communities they had come to care for.

The Target

The target was a major multinational corporation, known for its shady dealings and exploitation of South Africa's resources. It was the perfect mark—immense wealth, deep corruption, and a poor reputation among the public. Taking down this giant would be a poetic final move, a statement against the system they had fought from the shadows.

The heist would involve hacking into the corporation's central financial database, rerouting millions from its accounts into various offshore havens they controlled. It was a mission that would require the full strength of each member's skills, from Linda's tech expertise to Kabelo's financial wizardry.

The Perfect Plan

Planning took weeks. Linda studied the corporation's security infrastructure, poring over firewalls and encryption. Tumi, the psychology genius, mapped out the routines of key executives, learning their vulnerabilities and behavioral patterns. Kabelo constructed a complex financial web that would route the stolen funds across continents in milliseconds, ensuring the money would be untraceable. Bheka, the logistics expert, mapped out their escape routes, should anything go awry, and put failsafe plans in place in every major city they might need.

They dubbed it "Operation Exodus"—a symbolic farewell to the world of crime that had given them wealth, power, and respect but had also bound them in secrecy and danger. Each member knew their role precisely, and as the day of the heist approached, they went over the plan with military precision, preparing for every contingency.

The Heist

On the night of the operation, the team gathered in a secured location outside Johannesburg, where Linda remotely accessed the corporation's network. As her fingers flew over the keyboard, breaching layer after layer of security, Tumi and Bheka monitored every detail, double-checking escape plans and alternate routes. Kabelo remained poised with his bank of monitors, ready to initiate the rapid transfer of funds.

When Linda finally reached the inner sanctum of the corporation's finances, there was a quiet exhilaration in the room. This was it—the culmination of all their years in the game. With one click, Linda unlocked the vault, and Kabelo took over, inputting the coded commands that would trigger a massive, simultaneous sweep of accounts. In less than ten minutes, millions began to vanish from the corporation's coffers, redirected to a network of shell companies they controlled.

Just as the final transfer completed, an alarm sounded. Linda's face paled as she saw a notification: their activity had been detected, and law enforcement was on its way.

The Narrow Escape

Bheka sprang into action, calmly coordinating their exit strategy. Each team member had a carefully plotted route and disguise, and they dispersed like shadows, moving through Johannesburg with practiced precision. As police cars swarmed the area, Vuruvayi and his friends managed to evade capture through a network of allies and safe houses they had set up for just such an emergency.

Within hours, they were all safely out of the city, each taking separate paths to designated safe zones across South Africa. Once secure, they communicated through a private, encrypted channel, relieved that everyone had made it out unscathed.

The Legacy They Left Behind

The next day, news of the massive heist broke. The public reveled in the downfall of the corrupt corporation, while officials scrambled to respond. But for Vuruvayi and his friends, the heist marked their final bow. Each member of the crew used their cut of the fortune to establish funds for scholarships, healthcare facilities, and community development initiatives across South Africa, embedding their legacy in a way that would continue long after they were gone.

Though they disappeared from public view, Johannesburg—and indeed the country—would never forget them. To some, they were criminals, but to the communities who benefitted from their work, they would forever be legends, the unseen architects of a better South Africa.

Chapter 30: Legacy Left Behind

WITH THEIR FINAL SCORE behind them, Vuruvayi and his team dispersed, each choosing a quiet, hidden life in different parts of the world. They left South Africa as legends, their names whispered in both awe and relief, their true identities known only to each other and a select few. Each member had arranged to live comfortably, but they hadn't just left with their pockets full—they had left behind a legacy woven into the very fabric of Johannesburg and beyond.

Investments That Built Futures

The millions they had amassed were no longer just hidden wealth; it was fuel for change. Vuruvayi used his share to establish a network of scholarships that would support disadvantaged students from Johannesburg, Daveyton, and townships across South Africa. He knew what it was like to come from nothing, and he was determined that young people who showed promise would get the support he never had. Scholarships in fields like engineering, medicine, and education were offered under anonymous foundations, each bearing names inspired by his past and his team, ensuring their legacy would endure in ways that mattered.

Linda, the tech mastermind, set up tech hubs in townships across the country. These hubs were designed to offer free resources, training, and mentorship programs for youth interested in technology, coding, and cybersecurity. Each hub provided internet access, modern equipment, and even internships at reputable companies. As one of the most gifted hackers in South Africa's shadow history, Linda ensured that her legacy would uplift future generations who would use technology for positive change.

Community Centers, Health Clinics, and Housing

Bheka, the logistics expert, poured his resources into building community centers in underserved areas. These centers became places where children could learn, adults could access vocational training, and families could receive support services. He even arranged partnerships with local healthcare providers to offer free clinics, giving residents access to healthcare in places where it was scarce. To Bheka, the operation wasn't over until the people they had once shielded from danger could live safe, healthy lives.

Kabelo, with his financial acumen, created an affordable housing initiative. He invested in sustainable housing projects across Johannesburg, Durban, and Cape Town, providing affordable, quality homes for low-income families. He also set up financial literacy programs, teaching people about investments, savings, and homeownership. In time, Kabelo's initiatives transformed entire neighborhoods, creating pockets of opportunity that would uplift generations.

Unseen Heroes of Johannesburg

The transformation didn't go unnoticed. Johannesburg and its surrounding townships felt the impact of these mysterious benefactors in countless ways, from libraries stocked with books to youth centers filled with laughter and hope. Residents often wondered about the identity of these unseen heroes who had somehow turned fortunes around for those who needed it most. No one could say for sure, but many stories painted them as modern-day Robin Hoods, taking from the corrupt and giving back to those who had been left behind.

While the world knew little of their true identities, the crew's impact was undeniable. Stories circulated of how young lives were being changed, of how crime had diminished in certain areas thanks to education, opportunity, and hope.

A New Generation Inspired

Years later, Vuruvayi and his team's influence could still be felt. South Africa saw the rise of a generation of leaders, tech innovators, healthcare professionals, and educators who had been shaped by the opportunities that Vuruvayi's crew had made possible. Young people who had once been without hope now had access to a brighter future and spoke of giving back to the communities that raised them. For the team, this was the truest success, a legacy far more lasting than the money they'd taken or the power they'd wielded.

Though they had left the world of crime behind, Vuruvayi and his team watched from afar as the seeds they had planted grew. Each lived in quiet anonymity, with the knowledge that their work had not only changed their lives but had forever transformed the lives of those who followed. They had become more than mere shadows—they were part of South Africa's heart, its silent architects of a better tomorrow.

Ghosts of the Golden City

In Johannesburg's underworld, Vuruvayi and his team are masters of the perfect heist. Each member is a genius in their field—technology, finance, psychology, logistics—and together they target the city's most corrupt, dismantling empires from within. With every job, they build a reputation as modern-day Robin Hoods, using their stolen fortunes to transform South Africa's forgotten communities.

But as their influence grows, so does the risk. Pursued by law enforcement and shadowed by betrayal, they face a dangerous game where loyalty is fragile and mistakes are costly.

Ghosts of the Golden City is a high-stakes journey into the art of the heist, where ambition and redemption collide in the shadows of Johannesburg's glittering skyline.

Don't miss out!

Visit the website below and you can sign up to receive emails whenever Sibusiso Anthon Mkhwanazi publishes a new book. There's no charge and no obligation.

https://books2read.com/r/B-A-QNVAB-HLEGF

BOOKS 2 READ

Connecting independent readers to independent writers.

Did you love *Ghosts of the golden city*? Then you should read *Sisters of A cursed bloodline*[1] by Sibusiso Anthon Mkhwanazi!

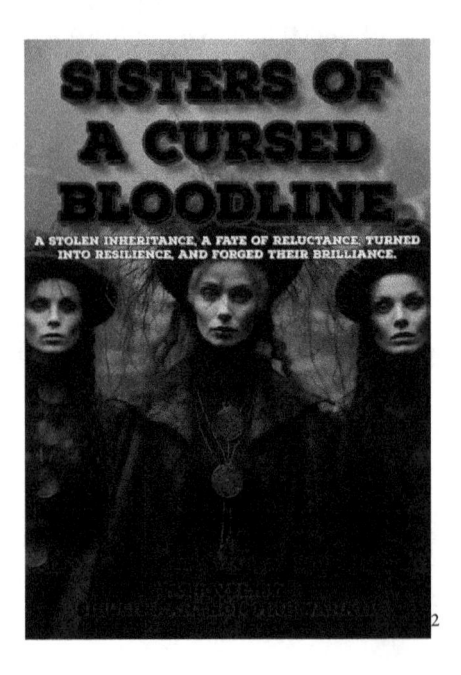

Three orphaned sisters, Balindile, Zandile, and Sthembile, lose their parents on the day of their birth and are taken in by a family with hidden motives. Exploited and neglected by those who should have protected them, the triplets grow up in a world of betrayal and hardship. Driven by anger and a deep desire to uncover the truth, they discover that their parents were victims of a dark family secret.

As they struggle to survive, the sisters face unimaginable challenges, including turning to prostitution to make ends meet. But just when their hope seems lost, a vivid dream of lottery numbers changes everything. Balindile takes a leap of faith, and they win millions, transforming their lives overnight.

---

1. https://books2read.com/u/mqnane

2. https://books2read.com/u/mqnane

Now wealthy, the triplets build a real estate empire, finding both success and fulfillment. But when their estranged families try to reconnect, they must confront the past and decide whether to forgive or to finally close the door on those who wronged them.

This is a powerful story of resilience, empowerment, and the bonds of sisterhood. As the sisters turn their pain into a lasting legacy, they show that true strength comes from within and that even the darkest beginnings can lead to the brightest futures.

Also by Sibusiso Anthon Mkhwanazi

Million-Dollar Decade
Resilience Beyond Pain
Resonance Of Hope
Cheating hearts to true love
The Dream Builders Of Daveyton
Before the Bible
Ink and Imagination
Becoming A Millionaire In South Africa
Leaders of the World
Mining In Africa
Origins of Language and Civilization
Vita Nova Centre
Sisters of A cursed bloodline
Witchcraft in Africa
Ghosts of the golden city

Milton Keynes UK
Ingram Content Group UK Ltd.
UKHW030747121124
451094UK00013B/893